Along Came a Black Bird

Along Came

Black Bird

ELIZABETH WILD

J. B. Lippincott   New York

Along Came a Black Bird

Library of Congress Cataloging-in-Publication Data
Wild, Elizabeth.
  Along came a black bird.

  Summary: Three young sisters and their pet crow
befriend a lonely boy from a neighboring farm and
discover some of the harsher realities of life.
  [1. Friendship—Fiction. 2. Family problems—
Fiction. 3. Sisters—Fiction. 4. Maine—Fiction]
I. Title.
PZ7.W64572A1   [Fic]   87–45882
ISBN 0–397–32293–3
ISBN 0–397–32294–1 (lib. bdg.)

With love, to Helen and Jane

Along Came a Black Bird

CHAPTER ONE

knew Beau Carney was a thief the first time I saw him, crouching down behind the magazines at the back of Muldoon's Drug Store. My sister Stephanie had sent me to Muldoon's to buy us some gum balls.

"Now, Louise, don't get those puny ones like you did last time," Stephanie said, pressing a quarter into my hand, "and save the purples for me."

With a flip of her ponytail my older sister ran off down Main Street to the post office. I didn't have a chance to remind her. Purple was my favorite too.

I hurried into the store thinking of gum balls. I liked the feel of my teeth cracking the hard outer shell and the soft plop of the bubble before it collapsed into my lips. Luscious fruity grape, red-hot cinnamon, cool mint green—my mouth was watering as I pushed open Muldoon's fly-splattered screen door.

The gum-ball machines were lined up at the back of the store beyond the magazines and birthday cards like a row of glittering treasure chests. I was fumbling in my pocket when my quarter slid out of my fingers, rolled around in a tight circle, and disappeared under the greeting-card stand.

Darn! I was in for it now. Stephanie would blow her top if I came back empty-handed.

I squeezed behind the card stand and got down on my hands and knees. I hoped nobody would catch me. You don't expect to see a ten-year-old girl crawling around on all fours like a baby. Not in public, anyway. In the dark I ran my fingers over the floorboards. The dust was thick as chicken feathers on the bare, splintery wood. Suddenly I realized somebody was standing not six feet away on the other side of the card display.

First I made out two beat-up sneakers. Then a pair of knobby ankles, and ragged pant legs that stopped six inches too soon. The person was standing on tiptoe. I figured he was peering over the top of the magazines toward the front of the store. Up front by the cash register Mr. Muldoon was shooting the breeze with two customers, arguing about Saturday's baseball game. The place smelled of Mr. Muldoon's stale cigar smoke and week-old popcorn.

I peeked out of my hiding place. The boy had his back to me. I guessed he was thirteen or fourteen, but tall for his age. His blue shirt was faded, the sleeves ripped through at the elbows. He had floppy yellow hair, cut as if somebody had plopped a bowl

4

over his head and snipped round the edge.

His body was completely still. But his hands moved steady as windshield wipers, pulling magazines off the shelf and sliding them noiselessly into a paper bag on the floor. The Muldoons' cat sat on a stack of newspapers at the end of the rack and peered at him lazily through half-open eyes. Her tail twitched.

Every so often the boy stretched up to make sure Mr. Muldoon wasn't watching. At first I thought maybe they had hired a new kid to sort through the magazines. But by the time he'd collected a good-sized stack of about twenty or so, it suddenly dawned on me. I was seeing a real live thief in action.

I tried to make myself small behind the card stand and wondered what to do. If I clammed up, Mr. Muldoon would lose a pile of magazines. But if I hollered, the kid might turn on me. What if they hauled me off to the police station as a witness and the kid came looking for me later? Then I'd really be in hot water.

Up front the men's voices droned on.

"Hey, Muldoon, Wilkins ain't been playing long. They just signed him in fifty-two, right? You're too hard on him. Give him a break! He's just a kid!"

"A break? He's draggin' the whole team right down the drain!" Mr. Muldoon protested. "They don't need Wilkins any more than a dog needs two tails!"

The men laughed. Mr. Muldoon chuckled at his

5

own joke. People said Mr. Muldoon had only two topics of conversation: no-good kids and baseball.

The cat jumped down lightly off the newspapers and brushed against the boy's leg. The boy was so nervous, for a minute I thought he'd leap right out of his skin. The cat's back was arched, and her tail curved like a question mark in the air. What should I do?

The kid's hands shook as he folded the paper bag shut, crouching down low to hide from the men up front. The back door was ajar just behind me. Any second he'd probably make a run for it.

Don't ask me where I got the nerve. As he darted for the doorway, I shot out my foot, pushing the wire card rack into his path. There was a deafening crash. The rack clattered to the floor right smack in front of him. Postcards fluttered in all directions. The boy clutched his knee. The bag spilled magazines at his feet.

"Hey! What's going on back there?" shouted Mr. Muldoon.

My heart was racing a mile a minute, and I got a sickish feeling in my stomach.

The boy picked himself up, scooped up an armload of magazines, and dashed out the door into the parking lot behind the store.

"Hey! Who's messing around back there?" bawled Mr. Muldoon, hurrying toward the back of the store as I crawled out from behind the display. His face was red as a lobster and his shirttails flapped behind. His friends were right on his heels.

"What's the meaning of this?" he demanded, frowning down at me, hands on his hips. The men set the card stand upright, sorting out the postcards and dusting them off before putting them back in the rickety wire rack.

"I don't know, Mr. Muldoon," I said. "You see, my quarter rolled under this stand a few minutes ago. . . ."

My voice trailed off. It had all happened so quickly, I could hardly think.

"Ain't you one of Dr. Berry's girls?" asked Mr. Muldoon.

"Louise. The second one," I stammered.

"I thought I saw somebody run out the back door," said Mr. Muldoon.

"Yes," I said, "there was a boy in here."

"Took something with him, did he?"

"I think he had some magazines," I said.

"Crummy, no-good hooligan . . ." muttered Mr. Muldoon. His face was purple.

"Well, who was he? Did you get a good look at him?"

"I've never seen him before," I said.

There was something in Mr. Muldoon's voice that made me uncomfortable. The veins in his neck stood out, and his eyes narrowed into slits.

"Well, what did he look like?"

7

I thought for a minute. Yellow hair and skinny legs flashed into my mind.

"He had black hair and was fat," I said. My heart skipped a beat.

"Black hair and fat?" echoed Mr. Muldoon. "Like Sonny Farrell?"

"Oh, no," I mumbled, wondering what ailed me. "I know Sonny. It definitely wasn't him."

"And you're sure you've never seen him before?"

"Never seen him before," I said. "I'm sorry."

What was the matter with me? I had just told a great big fat lie. Was I going nuts? I knew stealing was wrong. Mr. Muldoon deserved to make some money off his dumb magazines, even if he did hate kids. Maybe I was afraid the thief would get caught and have it in for me for telling on him. Or maybe it was his shaking. I just didn't want to turn him in.

Mr. Muldoon and the men went out to the parking lot to try to make sense of the scuff marks in the dirt.

"I could of swore there was a tall kid in the back of the store," I heard Mr. Muldoon saying. "Light-haired and skinny."

"But that Berry girl said black hair and fat. One of the Berry girls wouldn't lie to ya', Muldoon."

"I suppose you're right." Mr. Muldoon came back into the store scratching his head. "There's no tellin' what kids today will do. They'd rob me blind if I let 'em.

8

"Find your quarter?" asked Mr. Muldoon, walking by and not waiting for my answer.

"Nope, but that's all right. It was my fault. I guess it's gone for good." I followed him meekly to the front of the store. "Well, I'd better go now. My father said he'd be done at the office at three. I'm sorry about those magazines. I really am. I hope you find out who did it."

I was in an awful hurry to get out of there. Standing on the sidewalk, I took a deep breath. Suddenly I hoped I'd never have to set foot in Muldoon's Drug Store again. The clouds overhead were darker now. I drew my jacket around me as the first drops of rain fell in big gray polka dots on the pavement.

I wondered where the boy had gone. Like a lot of little Maine towns, Ellbridge is small, and everybody knows everybody else's business. If they don't, they try to find out. As I walked up Main Street, I stared at the people in the passing cars, but I didn't spot the kid. I remembered his hands going double quick, stuffing magazines in the bag. A box of candy and a bottle of nail polish had also tumbled out of the bag when it broke.

"Lou! Hurry up! It's starting to rain!"

Stephanie rolled down the window of the Jeep. Father put his medical bag into the backseat. I climbed into the Jeep and squeezed in beside Stephanie.

"What took you so long?" she demanded. "Where's the gum?"

"I lost my money under the card stand, so I couldn't buy anything."

"Didn't you look for it?"

"Sure, I looked for it. But it didn't turn up."

Stephanie groaned and rolled her eyes. She was almost thirteen, though sometimes she acted more like twenty. She had pretty brown eyes, a mouthful of braces. Her long hair was tied back in a neat ponytail that she flipped around a lot, especially when she was mad.

I took after Father's side of the family. I was short and had straight black hair. They used to call me Peewee, but now that I was older they didn't.

"Rats! I was dying for a piece of gum." Stephanie flicked her ponytail once or twice and settled back gloomily in her seat with her arms crossed, glaring out the window. She was annoyed with me, but I didn't care. I was used to it.

Father turned the key and started backing the Jeep out of the parking space. He was craning his neck to watch for the oncoming traffic when I saw a muddy red pickup driving past us. Its back bumper was nothing but rust. The boy from Muldoon's was sitting in the passenger seat.

"There he is!" I exclaimed in an excited whisper.

"Who?" said Stephanie, whirling around to get a better look.

"The boy in that truck that just went by."

"What are you talking about, Lou? What boy?"

10

The image of the boy grabbing his knee floated in my head. I wondered what it would be like if I got called in to be a witness. Squeezing my arm too tight, a scruffy policeman would usher me into a dark courtroom in the Ellbridge County Courthouse with wood paneling on the walls and a needle-nosed judge up front wearing a black robe. Mr. Muldoon would be surrounded by lawyers, all glaring at me, and the kid would be scowling at the floor.

"What boy are you talking about, Peewee?" said Stephanie impatiently.

"Oh, just some kid I saw when I was coming up the street just now," I murmured. "He had a really weird haircut, way too long."

"Oh, big deal," said Stephanie. She glanced at me suspiciously.

"And don't call me Peewee!" I snapped.

We pulled out onto Main Street and drove by the hardware store and the gas station. The red pickup was stopped at the light, right in front of us.

"Wonder who that is up ahead? Can you read what it says on the back of the truck?" asked Father.

My sister leaned forward, squinting at the truck. The rain was coming down steadily now. It was hard to get a good view.

"Carneys' Plumbing Service," she read slowly.

"Carneys'?" I said.

"Yeah, Carneys'," she said, looking at me with curiosity.

"You mean that truck belongs to the Carneys, the same Carneys that just moved in down the road from us?"

"So what's so strange about that?" Stephanie rolled her eyes. "That truck fits in perfectly with the rest of the stuff they've got in their yard."

I scrunched down low, praying the boy wouldn't turn around. To think that the thief lived right down the road from us. The next house over from the Farrells. I wondered if he had seen my foot in the drugstore. He was staring straight ahead. Neither person in the car turned around. I decided to wear my other pair of sneakers from now on.

"Carneys' Plumbing Service. That explains why they put the empty toilet out by the mailbox. To advertise the business," said Father.

Mother nearly died when she saw the toilet out front. She was hoping the new people would fix up the place. The Carneys' house was little and boxy, with a low, sagging roof and white paint peeling off the sides. The people who used to live there dumped a couple of rusted-out cars in the backyard, not to mention oil drums, a rotting picnic table, half a dozen bald tires, a roll of chicken wire, and a lot of other junk.

"I think they have a boy about your age, girls. That's what your mother said."

Soon after they had moved in, Mother had called to welcome them and learned they had a son.

12

"Name's Beauregard," continued Father absent-mindedly.

"Beauregard? What sort of dumb name is that?" said Stephanie.

"Southern probably," answered Father as the light changed.

The truck veered off to the right. I breathed a sigh of relief as the Carneys' truck disappeared over the crest of the hill. Beauregard Carney could have lived anywhere in Hanover County. And here he was, right next door. I wondered whether he had stolen stuff before he moved here. Maybe he had a police record somewhere. Father drove straight ahead.

"Hey! Where are we going?" said Stephanie.

"I thought you girls might like a little surprise," said Father. "A little something out of the ordinary before we go home."

"A surprise?" Stephanie and I chimed in at once.

"Are we stopping at the Dairy Queen for an ice cream?" I asked. I was relieved to get Beauregard off my mind.

"Father wouldn't take us there without Jennie. She'd have a fit," said Stephanie. Our sister Jennifer was five years old and was having her nap at home.

"I know! We're going to see the patient with the dog that plays the piano!"

"Not again. I hope not. It's a half-hour drive." Stephanie pressed her nose to the window and blew a row of steamy circles on the glass.

Father was concentrating on his driving. He was wiping the condensation off the windshield with one hand and steering the Jeep over the rain-slicked road with the other. The defroster was broken. I flopped back on the seat and swung my head back and forth to the steady rhythm of the windshield wipers.

Stephanie shot a disgusted look in my direction. "Stop doing that, Lou. It jerks the seat."

Father turned the steering wheel sharply.

"Hmmm. Think I'll drop by Dr. Butler's," he said.

"Oh, no," said Stephanie, throwing her head back against the seat in resignation. "This will take forever."

Dr. Butler was the only veterinarian in Ellbridge, and Father the only doctor. Saturday afternoons, if they weren't busy, they liked to get together and hash things over for an hour or two.

"What about the surprise?" I said.

"I won't forget the surprise, don't worry," called Father over his shoulder. He disappeared into the office.

The rain drummed down steadily on the Jeep. Stephanie drew a tic-tac-toe game on the window and started off with *X*s. I was stuck being an *O*. She won the first game and began making the lines for the second. Meanwhile I wrote "HI THERE" backward on my window so that it would read the right direction to somebody outside. Then we played twenty questions. Then we closed our eyes and tried to open them when we guessed Father would be coming out. It was getting pretty boring. Finally we just sat and listened to the rain.

"A kid's hairstyle shouldn't make you so nervous," said Stephanie suddenly.

"No, I guess it shouldn't."

"Then why did you act so weird about seeing him?"

"Weird?" I said.

"Yes, weird. Peculiar. Flaky. Bananas."

"Oh, come on, Stephanie. I didn't act like that."

"Sure you did. You almost sounded like you were scared of the kid."

"Oh," I said, licking dots on the window with my tongue.

The office door slammed and Father beckoned to us.

"Girls, come on in! Doctor Butler wants to show you something!"

Soon we were standing in the veterinarian's office. It felt good to be in out of the rain. Puddles formed under our wet sneakers. Rows of labeled glass bottles lined one wall of the room. Papers spilled off a desk onto the concrete floor. In the infirmary next door a few dogs howled and whimpered. A faint odor of medicine filled the air, though mostly it smelled like wet animal fur.

"How's everything, kids?" asked Dr. Butler in

his gravelly voice. "Your father thought you needed a little outing, is that it?"

Dr. Butler was a stringy old man with graying hair and laughing eyes. He towered over Father, who was short and bald. He followed us into the infirmary as Stephanie nudged me ahead of her down the narrow aisle of animal cages. A dog lying on a bed of clean newspaper thumped its tail as we walked past. He had a heavy plaster cast on his front leg.

"Hey! Isn't this Drummer, the Farrells' dog?" said Stephanie. She patted the dog lightly on the head, smoothing down the tiny tufts of fur over his sad brown eyes. The dog whined softly and licked her hand.

The Farrells lived halfway between us and the Carneys. They raised milk cows and stored their hay in our barn. Mr. Farrell had two sons, Sonny and Clarence, who had just graduated from high school.

"Some joker shot him by mistake," said Dr. Butler. "He'll be okay."

"Drummer got shot?"

"Trigger-happy nut," said Dr. Butler, shaking his head as he scratched behind the dog's ears. "Some blockheads will use anything for a target, whether it's hunting season or not."

We thumped Drummer on the back a couple of times before passing on to a yippy fox terrier, followed by a mangy long-haired cat. Dr. Butler pointed to a wire cage pushed into the back corner. Something black stirred inside.

"Now here's a little fellow your dad wanted you to see," said Dr. Butler, winking at Father, who grinned back.

We peered into the cage. There, pressed into the far corner, was a real live crow. He wasn't full grown— probably no more than ten inches from beak to tail. He cocked his head and looked at us, blinking in that funny way birds do, the bottom eyelid coming up to meet the top. I started to poke my finger through the wire grid work, but Stephanie yanked my arm away.

"Go ahead. He won't hurt," said Dr. Butler. "Just be careful of his wing."

"What's the matter with it?" I asked.

"Broken. He was brought in yesterday morning. He'd been out on the lawn half the night, dragging his wing behind him, making an awful racket."

"Will his wing be all right?" I asked.

"It's all fixed. In a week or two, he'll be as good as new."

Dr. Butler lifted the bird out of the cage and extended its wing for us to see. It was mended with a wooden tongue depressor and white adhesive tape.

"Want to hold him, Lou?"

The doctor settled the bird into my arms. I could feel his heart ticking like a watch. I wondered if the crow missed his mother.

"He's a baby, you know," continued the veterinarian. "Probably not more than four or five weeks old. The younger birds still have gray coloration on their backs."

He lifted the crow up to the bare light bulb to give us a better look.

"Let's put him back into the cage. You can take him out to the Jeep when you go."

Our mouths fell open in surprise. "Take him out to the Jeep?"

"Sure," said Dr. Butler. "Didn't your dad tell you?"

"You mean we're really taking him home with us?" asked Stephanie. Dr. Butler chuckled and Father grinned from ear to ear. This was the surprise.

The crow pulled himself to the front of the cage as if listening to the conversation. His eyes gleamed like bright black beads. When he opened his beak, the inside of his mouth looked as soft as red velvet.

Dr. Butler rummaged through the drawers of his desk and finally handed Father a sheaf of papers about raising wild birds.

"What does he eat?" asked Stephanie.

"Eat? Lord, that guy will eat anything. How are you fixed for dog food?"

"Oh, we have plenty of dog food," said Stephanie. We had a dog named Micky at home.

Father and Dr. Butler talked some more about the crow while Stephanie and I knelt down in front of the cage. The crow turned his head away.

"He's embarrassed that somebody is staring at him," I giggled.

"No, he's scared," said Stephanie. "I can hardly wait to get him home and start teaching him stuff. Crows are supposed to be very intelligent birds."

"He'll make a fine pet," said Dr. Butler. "Support his feet when you lift him up for a few days so he won't try to flap his wings."

Father put the cage under his arm. We thanked Dr. Butler and headed for the Jeep.

"And keep him away from those crazy hunters!" Dr. Butler called from his office door. "I don't need another Drummer!"

All the way home we kept the crow safe on the seat between us. He didn't make a single sound.

CHAPTER TWO

"**B**lack chicken?" said Jennie.

She was just up from her nap. Her cheeks glowed like polished pink apples, and her hair was matted in silky clumps.

Mother put down the laundry basket and came over to inspect. We already had quite a few animals—silver-laced wyandotte chickens, pheasants, bantams, guinea hens, not to mention our dog and a pregnant cat, Redhead. Last year we'd hatched a sea gull in the incubator, but he left us as soon as he could fly. Jennie had cried for two days solid.

"Will this bird learn to fly?" asked Jennie.

"Sure. He'll figure it out," I said. "Instinct. When he makes up his mind to it, he'll take off."

"Take off? For good? And not come back, like Buffy?" A worried look crept into her eyes. Buffy was the sea gull. He had taken several weeks to learn how to fly, taxiing down our driveway over and over like an airplane just before lift-off. One day he got the hang of it and never came back.

"Of course he won't fly off," said Stephanie. "He'll be so used to us by then, he'll have to stick around."

She got a spoon out of the kitchen drawer and began opening a can of dog food with the can opener. Then she knelt down on the floor next to the cage.

"*Ark! Yipple! Quark! Scritch-bibble! Aaaaaaack!*"

The crow had spotted his dinner.

"*Ricket! Ratch! Cartle-cartle-cartle!*"

"He's starving!" said Jennie anxiously. "Quick! Feed him!"

The crow stretched his mouth wide open and Stephanie shoveled gobs of dog food down his throat. His head jerked back like a hammer as he struggled to swallow each spoonful. He ate the whole can before he stopped opening his beak.

"Don't worry, Jen. He likes us," said Stephanie. "I can tell he's used to us already. Didn't you see the way he opened his mouth?"

Jennie looked doubtful.

"Come on. We'll take him around the farm. You'll see. He'll get attached for sure."

It had stopped raining. The sun was out and the fog had lifted. The granite mountains of Mount Desert Island sprawled across the horizon like flattened gray bubbles. We carried the crow across the road from the white farmhouse to our big red barn, and then down to the clam flats of the Worden River beyond that. It was low tide. Rainwater dripped from the trees, and the air smelled of seaweed and pinecones.

"Want to take our crow over and show the new neighbors?" said Jennie.

I pretended I didn't hear. The last person in the world I wanted to see was Beauregard Carney.

"I said, do you want to go over to the new people's house?" said Jennie a little louder.

"Well, I suppose we could," said Stephanie. "Maybe we should call first though."

"We can't go over there," I said, feeling myself turning red. "The crow's wing isn't healed yet, and besides, it's too close to supper. They might be eating dinner. We can't barge in on them like that."

Stephanie shrugged her shoulders.

"We've got to fix up a box for him for overnight. Father says he should be in a warm place with a hot water bottle, at least at first. I think we should take him home right this minute."

"Okay, okay," said Stephanie. "After he learns to fly, Jen. Maybe then we'll walk over."

She eyed me with suspicion.

"Something is bugging you about the Carneys, Lou. You can't fool me. Come on. What gives?"

"Nothing," I said. "Hey, the crow is shivering. I'm going back to the house."

After supper that night, when Jennie was in bed, Father spread out Dr. Butler's wild bird papers on the kitchen table. They were mostly articles written by people who had kept birds as pets themselves. My article told about a crow who had lived with his owner for twenty-five years.

"That's probably because they got him right out of the nest," said Father. "If you get a crow more than two weeks old, like ours, you can't count on him to stay around more than one season."

"Don't tell Jennie," I murmured, thinking about Buffy again.

Mother's article told about different personalities of crows. Some birds turn out to be friendly and some are mean as all get-out. Some are meek and fearful, and some turn out to be real pests.

"Listen to this," said Stephanie in an excited voice, looking up from the page with her finger following the words along. "This says that farmers shoot crows because they pull up the young corn shoots in their fields just after they're planted. The crows like the soft kernel under the soil."

"Shoot crows?" I said. I looked at the crow's broken wing and wondered exactly what had happened. Farmers might take aim at ordinary crows, but would they shoot a pet crow? In a field speckled with crows, how could a farmer tell a pet crow from a wild one? From a distance they'd all look the same.

"Well, April is way too early to worry about sprouting corn," said Mother reassuringly. "Besides, the Farrells don't raise corn. They raise cows."

I tried not to think about it. Imagine our crow

helplessly dodging the flash of a gun. I wondered if the Carneys would plant corn or if Beauregard had a gun. Or the Farrell boys, what if they decided to take a few potshots just for the heck of it? What about Drummer? Thank goodness the boys weren't home all that much. They had jobs up north at a lumber mill.

The clock struck nine. In the living room Father and Mother settled into their chairs with the newspaper. The fire hissed and crackled in the wood stove. Redhead, our cat, came out from behind the wood box and rubbed her fur against my pant leg, lighting up the dark with tiny sparks of electricity. Upstairs I could hear Stephanie running bathwater. The crow's cage was silent. He was leaning against the hot water bottle we'd fixed up for him.

"Sweet dreams, little crow!" I whispered. "Don't worry, we'll never let anybody get you. I promise!"

The crow's black eyes sparkled. I made tiny cawing noises, trying to sound like a crow's mother. Then I went upstairs to bed.

The next day we built a small outdoor cage out of chicken wire and overturned an old wooden crate at one end for shelter. Then Father nailed together some boards for two signs. We painted them white. As soon as the paint was dry, we stenciled in neat black letters: PLEASE DON'T SHOOT OUR PET CROW. We posted them along the road. People coming from either direction would be sure to see them.

"So when is he going to be able to fly?" asked Jennie for the fiftieth time. She was sure he would leave as soon as he could get off the ground.

"Let's think of a good name for him," I said, trying to change the subject. "How about Blackie?"

"No, too ordinary," said Stephanie.

"Cinders?"

"Fairy-talish."

"Midnight?"

"Too horsey."

"Well, *you* think of something then," I said.

"I already have," said Stephanie. "We're calling him Crowberry."

"Crowberry?"

"It's perfect. Our last name is Berry, right? And Crow isn't a cutesy pet. So we can't give him a cutesy name."

I practiced saying the name a few times. Crowberry wasn't half bad.

"Besides, I've already tried it out on him and he likes it," she said. "Watch this.

"Here, Crowberry. Here, Crowberry!" Her voice was halfway between a hiccup and a yodel.

The crow sat motionless and stared at her.

"See? He likes it. Otherwise he would have turned his head the other direction." Stephanie knew an awful lot about everything.

For a week Crowberry stayed in his pen, hopping about, stretching his wings, and hobbling over to see us when we knelt by the side of the cage. When a few of his feathers fell out, Dr. Butler told us to hide some vitamin pills in balls of dog food. But Crowberry was smart. He picked out the bright yellow capsules, and later we found them buried in little holes around the edges of the pen.

After that we tried feeding him a variety of different stuff, like cheese, crackers, baked potato skins, bread, and sugar cubes. Jennie and I collected a bunch of bugs and worms from the garden. If it didn't wiggle, Crowberry would eat it. Father butchered a chicken for Sunday dinner and we gave the insides to Crow. Liver, gizzard, intestines, and fat—he wolfed them down in one huge slurp. It turned your stomach to watch. Soon the feathers stopped falling out.

Finally Dr. Butler told Father he could take off Crow's splint. Stephanie held him a few inches off the ground.

"Okay, Crow, it's time to fly. Now flap those wings," she ordered.

She let go. Crow settled limply on the grass.

"Jen, get the dog food. Okay, Crow. No fly, no food! You hear?"

Jennie rattled the spoon against the side of the can. The crow crouched down. Then Stephanie grabbed the can and, climbing up on a fence post to see if Crow would try to follow, rattled it again. The bird was still as a statue.

"Birdbrain!" yelled Stephanie. "I've got a better idea, Lou. Meet me out in the barn in your Halloween costume."

"My Halloween costume?"

"Don't ask questions. Just go and put it on."

There was no use arguing with my sister. I hurried to the back closet and pulled out my bat costume. It had a large black cape and a black felt bag with eye holes cut into the front. I had glued two ivory piano keys under its nose—a bat with buckteeth. I won a prize for best costume at the Ellbridge Jaycees Halloween party back in first grade, but that had been four years ago, and by now the costume was getting a little ratty.

"Now, Lou, climb up there and act birdish."

Stephanie pointed over our heads to the platform of baled hay almost at the very top of the barn. By climbing up the bales of hay stacked in ledges on one side, you could reach the platform and grab the heavy knotted rope that served as a swing. Down below, the barn floor was heaped with loose straw several feet deep. The idea was to take a flying leap off the platform like a trapeze artist in the circus, letting go of the rope when you were far out over the cushion of hay below. We'd done it lots of times before.

"Okay, Crow. It's your last chance," shouted Stephanie, holding the bird up to watch. "Pay attention!"

"This is stupid," I said, climbing up to the platform. "This is the stupidest idea I ever heard of."

I gripped the rope between my knees and pushed off. The cape whooshed out behind me. I could hear Stephanie lecturing the crow. But I couldn't see a thing because the black bat head had slipped down over my eyes.

"You're not cawing, Lou," yelled Stephanie down below. "You have to rattle the can and caw at the same time!"

"I can't!" I cried. The rope slipped through my knees, and a moment later I bounced down onto the hay.

"Oh, for goodness' sake. Let me try it!" said Stephanie, setting Crowberry down on the floor. I handed her the costume and the dog food. Stephanie scrambled quickly up the bales to the top.

"Now watch me!" she commanded.

She flung herself into the emptiness of the dusty barn. The black cape swelled behind her. She rattled and cackled like a madwoman.

"Caw! Clatter-clatter! Caaaaaawwwww! Clickety-rattle! Caw! Caw! Caw!" She was swinging like a giant pendulum.

"You sound like a sick turkey!" I hollered. Jennie began to giggle.

"Hold him up high, Lou. Make sure he's watching!"

I turned to the spot where Stephanie had left

Crowberry. It was empty.

"Where did you leave Crow, Stephanie?" I called up.

"Right there by the door. I put him right there on a little pile of straw."

"Well, he's not there now!"

"What?"

"He's gone."

"He's got to be there. I just put him down. In that straw."

Stephanie let go of the rope and plunged downward into the hay. From behind the barn Jennie screamed in excitement. We raced outside. She was pointing at the barn roof.

There perched at the highest point was Crowberry, twisting his head around to survey the barnyard like a lordly black prince.

"You're not a birdbrain after all, Crow!" shouted Jennie. "You're very, very smart!"

"See? I told you it would work," said Stephanie, flashing her braces in a toothy grin. "His first flight, and you two completely missed it."

She shook her head, untied the bat cape, and crossed the road to the house. I shaded my eyes against the sun and squinted up at the tiny figure on the barn roof. His beak was open. It looked to me like Crowberry was having a good laugh.

CHAPTER THREE

*E*ach day Crowberry discovered something new. At first it was dive-bombing the chickens. Next it was pulling the flag off the mailbox. Then it was swinging on the clean laundry on the clothesline and teasing Micky, our dog, by flying just over his head, barely out of reach.

"This bird is a pain in the neck!" said Mother when she discovered Crow carefully pulling apart her tulips.

Crow could unravel a loose thread on a towel and worry the button on a hat till it hung by a thread. He'd swoop down on our marbles game and scoop up a marble in his beak, flying over the field to drop it in the grass. And he loved to hide things—bits of bright-colored paper, beads, or little white stones. Our crow wasn't fearful, or ornery, as the magazine article had said he might be. He was a plain and simple nuisance.

Mornings he sat outside our bedroom window, rapping on the glass to wake us up. The minute we got home from school we called him in a whooping singsong and waited for the tiny black dot to appear on the horizon. Soon he dropped down, planting his feet on our shoulders, arching his wings for a final flap before folding them in to his sides. At night he retreated to the top branches of the old pine behind the house. He stopped coming to us for food.

Stephanie had promised Jennie we'd take him over to the Carneys' after he learned to fly, but something happened first. Beauregard got caught.

This time it was at the A&P grocery store, three doors down from Muldoon's. We heard about it from Marty Jenkins at school. Her father runs the store.

Saturdays they lock up the place at five o'clock. Usually everybody goes home. But on this particular Saturday Mr. Jenkins stayed behind to check on some electrical wiring in the basement. When he came upstairs, there was Beauregard Carney, caught red-handed with a box of groceries and a half dozen bottles of cough syrup.

Marty's father called the police, but they wouldn't arrest Beauregard because he was underage. They figured he was hungry and trying to get tight on the medicine, that's what Marty said. When Mr. Carney showed up on the scene, he chewed Beauregard out something awful.

Somebody wrote up the story for the "Police Blotter" column of the *Ellbridge American*, not mentioning any names, of course. I wondered whether Mr.

Muldoon read it, or if he ever put two and two together and figured out that it was the same kid who ran off with his magazines.

So we didn't go over to the Carneys' after all. When Jennie asked why not, we made up some dumb excuse to shut her up.

School was almost over for the year. It was starting to get hot. Redhead had her kittens, six in all. The marigolds were in full bloom in the Carneys' toilet. One warm June evening we had our piano recital, and Patty Bromley's father fainted right in the middle of it. Ellery Clifford never missed a note of "Minuet in G," even though Mr. Bromley was out cold on the floor in the back row. Too many candles for a stuffy living room, everyone said as they carried him out.

At church they were getting ready for the final Sunday school picnic at Lawrence Point. The Point is about three miles from our house. It has a pebbly beach right on the ocean where you can find snails and mussels and sea urchins under the seaweed.

On the day of the picnic Mother suggested we drive directly to the park instead of driving into town to meet up with the Sunday school group, turning around, and driving all the way back out to the picnic. So we piled our stuff in the Jeep, waved goodbye to Crow, and started off.

As we passed the Farrells', the cows were chewing their cuds and swishing away flies with their tails.

Drummer was trotting down the dirt road that ran into an old dump, hidden back in the woods across from the Farrells' barn. His leg must have healed. There was no sign of a limp.

At the Carneys', two people were working in the field behind the house, turning over their garden. The ground was dark and moist and carved into rows. There was even a makeshift scarecrow. One person tossed rocks into the bushes while the other worked the shovel. They straightened their backs and watched as we drove past.

"There's the new boy!" exclaimed Jennie.

I looked over her head. It was Beauregard all right, tall and skinny, leaning on his shovel.

Stephanie sat bolt upright and looked straight ahead.

"Don't stare!" she ordered. "I'm not going to get caught staring at Beauregard Carney!"

"Why not?" asked Jennie.

"Because he's a juvenile delinquent! That's why not!"

"Now, Stephanie," interrupted Mother, "you have never even met Beauregard."

Beauregard didn't go to school in Ellbridge with us, because officially he lived in the next town over. So we never saw him on the bus. The town line was halfway between the Carneys' and the Farrells'.

"Mother," groaned Stephanie, "don't you read the paper? He's not a nice person! He's a terrible person. He steals and gets drunk. Marty says he

33

probably takes hubcaps and sneaks into movies and tortures animals and starts fires—"

"And you believe all Marty's stories, do you?"

"It's not just Marty. That's what her father and Mr. Muldoon said."

Mother raised her eyebrows and Stephanie shut up. We were quiet the rest of the way to Lawrence Point. Jennie and Stephanie each took a side of the road and counted to see which had the most houses, then the most clotheslines, then a grand prize if you saw somebody actually hanging out the wash. I watched the moving shadow of the car against the grassy banks along the roadside.

When we got to the park, most of the Sunday school kids were down on the beach skipping stones and looking for jellyfish. We helped Mother unload the car. Then we raced off to play with our friends.

Soon we caught a whiff of smoke from the charcoal. The kids drifted back from the beach, their pockets loaded with crab shells and empty sand dollars. The fathers had pushed together tables under a picnic shelter, and the little kids were circling them with fists full of plastic forks and spoons. I was starving.

Our minister, Mr. Munson, was roasting the hot dogs on the grill. Judging from his size, I guessed he'd enjoyed quite a few hot dogs before in his life. The kids called him Winnie behind his back because he reminded us of a big, friendly teddy bear. We liked him because he didn't yell if you played tag in Sunday school.

Everyone gathered by the picnic shelter, dished up some Jell-O salad, cole slaw, baked beans, and potato chips, grabbed a hot dog at the grill, and found a place at a table. A hush fell as we waited for Mr. Munson to say grace. The sooner he started, the sooner we could eat.

"Dear friends, on this beautiful June day, let us be eternally thankful for the blessings our Lord has seen fit to bestow upon us, for the friendships we have made, and for our families, near and far away . . ."

Out of the corner of my eye I could see the boy across the table slide a pickle off his plate and sneak it into his mouth.

"Let us always be mindful of those less fortunate than we . . ."

A fly discovered my potato chips. My stomach was growling.

"And may we come to know and love all creatures in God's wonderful kingdom—"

"*Cutt-ratchety-ratchety-ratch!*"

"To increase our understanding of His goodness—"

"*Clippet-squirr-caaawww!*"

Mr. Munson broke off in mid sentence. We looked up to see what could be making such a weird noise.

There was Crowberry! He was sitting on a roof beam at the far end of the picnic shelter, his mouth open, jawing and cackling like nobody's business. Everybody started to laugh.

Mr. Munson went into high gear, full speed ahead. "Bless this food to our use and us to thy service. Amen!"

"*Craawwww!*" said Crow.

Stephanie hurried out on the grass with a bunch of Sunday school kids and called Crow to sit on her shoulder. He was gobbling bits of hot dog from anyone who would feed him.

"He must have followed the car," Mother apologized to Mr. Munson. "That bird treats us to one surprise after another. I had no idea he ever left our farm."

Crow flew over to Mr. Munson's shoulder and spit out a mouthful of chewed-up hot dog on his sleeve. Mother looked horrified, but the minister chuckled.

"A new first," he said with a grin, dabbing at his sleeve with a wadded-up napkin. "Dear Lord, may I be eternally grateful for the bounty I have just received."

After lunch Stephanie and I put Crowberry through his paces. He played tug-of-war with the jump rope and tried to catch sticks tossed up to him. He soared out over the ocean and zoomed in for a landing on Stephanie's shoulder. After a while he got bored and watched the relay races and baseball game from the top of a nearby tree.

"Mother, will he fly back with us?" Jennie was

starting to worry. Since we had gotten him, Crow had never been away from home, at least not that we knew about.

"Let's keep our fingers crossed," said Mother.

We loaded up for the trip back. Stephanie suggested we roll down the windows and call out, "Here, Crowberry!" all the way home. Mother drove slowly and pulled the car to the side of the road now and then to make sure Crow was with us. After a few minutes he would settle on a telephone wire just ahead of the car or even perch on the hood.

"I feel like a jerk hollering out the window like this," said Stephanie as we approached the Carneys'. "I'm quitting."

"Please keep stopping, Mother," Jennie pleaded, "until we get home. Please. If Crow gets lost, I'll die!"

That's how it happened that we stopped a few hundred feet from the Carneys' and saw Beauregard with his shotgun, his back to the road, shooting tin cans off the top of the scarecrow.

"Crow's in trouble!" Jennie screamed. "That boy has a gun. Don't stop!"

"Hush, it's all right. He's just doing target practice," said Mother.

I peered out the back window, a lump like a goose egg growing in my throat.

Look out, Crow! I thought. There's danger below!

I crossed the fingers of both hands. Mother pushed

the gas pedal to the floor, and we pulled out onto the road without waiting to see if Crow was with us or not. When we got home, we could still hear the popping of Beauregard's gun in the distance. Anxiously we scanned the sky. Seconds later Crow sailed onto the roof of the house.

"He made it! He made it! He didn't get lost and he didn't get shot! He's safe!" Jennie was beside herself. Her eyes sparkled with tears. Crow dropped down by her feet and strutted about as if nothing had happened.

After that we realized that we couldn't keep Crow at home. If we went out in the car, there was always a chance he might chase us. So we got in the habit of looking for him overhead. Once we thought he followed us into Ellbridge. We weren't sure it was Crow because he stayed up on the weathervane of the courthouse and didn't come down even when we called. It might have been some other crow.

Every day the splatter of gunshot from the Carneys' grew more ominous. But even worse, the corn was sprouting in the field behind their house, tiny green shoots in neat rows, just the kind crows love to pull up looking for the juicy kernel under the soil.

Whenever the gun went off, we hurried outside to make sure Crow was safe. We checked his favorite haunts—the pine tree, the barn roof, the windowsill. If he wasn't there we fanned out over the fields and along the riverbank, calling until we were hoarse.

Jennie fought back her tears. Finally the tiny black speck appeared in the sky. Then there was hugging and laughing and carrying on, while Crow strutted about happily in our midst. It happened a half dozen times at least.

As the Carneys' corn inched higher, whole flocks of crows settled in their field. You didn't have to be a brain to figure out that, sooner or later, Beauregard was going to hit his target.

In my mind I could see Crow clamping his beak shut on the tender shoot, bracing his feet, and tugging until the roots snapped and he hurtled backward. Then Beauregard taking careful aim, pulling the trigger, and *BAM!* Perhaps other crows in the flock lifted from the ground as a single body. But one helpless crow was left fluttering in the furrow, black wings beating between new green rows in a desperate struggle to survive. What if that one crow was ours?

It's funny how you can solve a big problem while you're drifting off to sleep. That's when I figured out what to do. By morning I had it all planned out. Lifting my head from the pillow, I could see the sky, a faint yellow stripe in the east behind the mountains. Stephanie's breathing rose and fell in steady rhythm. In the darkness I pulled on my blue jeans and an old shirt, and tiptoed out of the bedroom. The floorboards creaked under my feet.

The air outside was cold, and the dew made my

sneakers wet. It was just light enough to see where I was going. Venus hung bright and low over the horizon. I crossed the road to the barn. There wasn't a moment to spare.

In the dark I groped for the hook on the wall where Father hung the empty chicken feed bags. A few unused feed troughs clattered noisily as I stumbled around feeling for the full grain sack. At first I plunged my hand into the powdery chicken mash, but luckily, right next to it was the dried corn. I scooped handfuls of the hard grains into the sack until it was almost too heavy to lift. When I had as much as I could carry, I slung the bag over my shoulder and started down the road to the Carneys'.

I guessed it was five thirty. Beauregard would certainly be sound asleep. I passed our DON'T SHOOT sign glowing white in the half dark. The Farrells' house was next, but there was no sign of life there. The road into the dump looked like an empty black hole.

A truck, its headlights on, came up behind me and tooted. I froze in my tracks. Would they hear the horn at the Carneys'? The truck rattled on. The Carneys' windows stayed dark. My fingers were frozen, and I shifted the bag from one shoulder to the other. I had to get there before the Carneys got up.

Just past the marker for the town line I turned off the main road and struck out through the alder bushes. My plan was to cut in through the tangle of brush so that I would come out at the far end of the Carneys' cornfield. I tried to keep low so nobody would see me. Once I stumbled over an old stump, but I held the grain sack tight so none spilled out. I shielded my face with my arm to keep the alder branches from slicing into my eyes. My jeans were sopping wet to the knees.

If I was lucky, I'd fool both Crow and Beauregard. Pretty soon I could see the back door of the Carneys' old white farmhouse. In the dark I could barely make out the even rows of young, green corn shoots.

I knew I should have told somebody my plan, but for some reason, I just didn't. It was too late now anyway. Reaching my hand into the grain bag, I grabbed a handful of corn and threw it in the grass at the side of the field. Then I walked a few paces and tossed out some more.

It was a trick. If I put corn all the way around the edge of the garden, Crowberry wouldn't waste his time eating the seedlings but would gobble up the stuff I was putting out instead. I would only have to keep it up for a couple of weeks because after that the plants would be too big for him to handle. And if I scattered it far enough away, in the bushes and woods that surrounded the cornfield on three sides, Beauregard might not see our crow at all when he came over to eat.

I figured I'd have to get pretty close to their house because the corn patch was practically at their back door. I had worked myself around the far edges and was just coming up along one side to the place where their cornfield turned into backyard when I heard a door slam. A dog began to bark.

I was so frightened, I couldn't move. A light went on in the house. The door slammed again. Footsteps raced across the gravel. Someone turned on the headlights of the red pickup. Over the dog's frantic barking, a deep voice shouted.

"Who's out there?"

CHAPTER FOUR

I hear you out there!" boomed the voice behind the headlights. "If you don't want no trouble, you better come on out!"

My heart was in my mouth. If only I could be back at home tucked in safely under the covers.

"Hey, did ya' hear me? You come out here before I call the sheriff!"

If I ran now, that snarling dog would sink his teeth into the seat of my pants. Somebody might get out a gun. I didn't have any choice. I stood up, dropped the empty grain sack by my feet, and walked into the full beam of the headlights.

"Hey, Pa. It's just a kid!"

The lights were blinding. The dog was growling and straining at the leash.

"Now why in God's name would somebody be prowling around at six o'clock in the morning. If this ain't the craziest—"

"Hey, Pa, I think it's one of them girls from next door," called Beauregard from the porch. He was tugging on his shirt. The dog was barking furiously.

"Shut up, Bozo, ya' damn fool!" shouted the man.

Beauregard swatted the dog and dragged him by the collar to the porch steps, where he tied him up. Mr. Carney climbed out of the truck and pulled me toward him, clamping his big hand on my shoulder like a vise and squinting into my face. His bushy eyebrows looked like two woolly bear caterpillars inching across his forehead.

"You got some explainin' to do, young lady. Now come on into the house. I'm going to get on the phone to yer daddy right this minute."

I followed the Carneys up the rickety steps into the house. I was in a real tight spot. I couldn't tell them what I was doing, because if he knew why I'd come over, Beauregard might try twice as hard to get Crowberry. You can't trust juvenile delinquents.

"All right, young lady, what's yer phone number?" asked Mr. Carney, lifting the receiver and staring at me with curiosity. In the house he didn't look nearly as scary as in the dark driveway. He was short and wiry, and his eyes twinkled.

I told him each number slowly, and he repeated it to the telephone operator at the other end of the line.

"Hello, Doc?" he said, shouting into the receiver. "Listen, Doc. This is Francis Carney next door. Yeah, Frank, yer new neighbor. Listen, Doc. You're not going to believe this, but I got one of yer girls

44

standing in my kitchen this very minute."

There was a pause. I could hear Father's voice on the other end of the line.

"Which one? Hold on."

He cupped the receiver in his hand. His fingernails were caked with dirt.

"What's yer name?" he asked.

"Louise," I said, staring at the floor. Half a dozen patterns of linoleum scraps were pieced together to cover the kitchen floor.

"It's Louise. I don't know why she come over," Mr. Carney continued. "I asked her, but she ain't talking."

I glanced around the kitchen. The place was pretty bare. They had a calendar tacked up on the wall, a greasy-looking armchair in the corner, and some old rags stuffed around the cracks in the window. There was a half-chewed dog bone lying under the table and a bare light bulb hanging down from the ceiling. A shotgun was propped against the wall.

"Okay, Doc," said Mr. Carney. "See you in a few minutes. Right-o." He hung up.

"Now, young lady," said Mr. Carney, leaning over me, "suppose you tell us how you happened to be out in my backyard at this time of the night."

His eyebrows danced up and down like dragonflies over a pond. They sat perfectly still over his twinkling eyes. Then all of a sudden they shot straight up or darted way down. It was comical.

45

My mind searched for an answer that would keep Mr. Carney happy.

"Well, I guess I must have been walking in my sleep."

"Sleepwalking!" roared Mr. Carney.

I could feel myself turning red as a rooster's comb.

"Well, I never! You mean you got yourself dressed while you was sound asleep and come walking a half mile in the pitch black. . . ."

He tossed back his head and laughed. "We've heard some tall tales in our travels, ain't we, Beau, but this takes the cake. Don't be scared, honey," he added, "we'll get you back under them covers safe and sound."

I managed a weak smile. In the room off the kitchen someone started coughing like crazy. The smile faded from Mr. Carney's face.

"Frank! Please come in here! What's going on?" a hoarse voice called. It sounded like that of an old woman. Mr. Carney's eyebrows took a nosedive and leveled off into a frown.

"Coming, Lillian," he muttered as he shuffled out of the room and shut the door behind him.

Beauregard perched on a stack of old newspapers and scowled. He didn't look at me straight on exactly, just cast a glance in my direction every so often. Bozo whined to come in. Beauregard opened the back door and untied his leash. The dog growled as he sniffed at my shoes.

"He won't hurt," Beauregard grunted. "Just don't move sudden."

I sat like a statue and didn't say a word. Beauregard picked up wood chips off the floor and shot them into a yellow plastic dog dish. I stared at his bony ankles, remembering the last time I'd seen them, at Muldoon's.

On the other side of the closed door we could hear the muffled voices of Mr. Carney and the woman. They were talking back and forth about something, I couldn't tell what. At one point I thought he said, "It's your only chance, Lillian." Then the coughing drowned him out. Beauregard looked up at me.

"Ma's sick," he said, still pitching wood chips.

"I'm sorry to hear that," I said. "She sounds pretty bad."

"She is," said Beau.

The dog pricked up his ears. Father must be coming down the road. A minute or two later the wheels of the Jeep crunched on the gravel driveway and a couple of car doors slammed. Mr. Carney came out of the bedroom muttering under his breath.

"I'll be gol-darned if I know what to do."

Beauregard followed him with his eyes. Mr. Carney plastered a stiff smile on his face as he opened the door.

"Mrs. Berry, Doctor, come on in. Yer girl is right here."

For the first time all morning, I suddenly felt like

47

crying. Maybe it was the worried way Mother came running over and put her arms around me or Father's puzzled frown as he came into the room. I tried to hold back the sob welling up in my throat.

"Lou," said Mother, "are you all right, dear? What in the world made you come over to the Carneys'?"

I bit my lip. "I guess I was walking in my sleep, Mother. I don't know."

Mother's eyes searched my face. I blinked back the tears.

"We've caused the Carneys enough trouble for one day. Let's say good-bye and head back home," said Mother, throwing an apologetic glance at Mr. Carney, then returning her worried gaze to me. Mr. Carney cleared his throat loudly.

"Gee, Doc, I should have called you earlier—"

"Earlier?" said Father. "Six o'clock seems plenty early enough to me."

"Oh, no, I didn't mean about yer girl."

Mr. Carney coughed a couple of times and then began again.

"Say, Doc, you see, what I meant was, I know it's early in the mornin' and everthing, but I wonder . . ."

He shifted from one foot to the other. Mother and Father looked at him with interest. Mr. Carney seemed as nervous as a cat with wet feet.

"So long as you're here, if you could take a look at my wife. She's not feeling too good."

Father and Mother exchanged a quick glance.

"Sure thing, Frank. What seems to be the trouble?"

"I can't pay ya' right now, Doc," said Mr. Carney. "But I'd sure appreciate it if you could check her out. She's been coughin' like crazy."

"How long has this been going on?" asked Father.

"Oh, you know, a day or two. A week, maybe. Yes, maybe even two weeks, now that I think of it."

"More like two months, Pa," said Beauregard softly. "It's been two months at least."

"Oh, yeah, that's right, Beau. I guess it has been that long," said Mr. Carney, rubbing his chin and frowning.

"I'll get my bag and be right back," said Father.

"I sure do thank you for this, Mrs. Berry," said Mr. Carney. "Any plumbing jobs over there at the house?"

"Oh, no, don't think of the money," said Mother. "You must be very worried about your wife, if it's gone on this long."

"I've been trying to get her over to see Doc, but she's stubborn as a mule. She don't want to spend the money, you know? It gets to a point where she don't have no common sense about it. I mean, if you're sick, you're sick, right? You gotta call the doc."

Mr. Carney scratched his grizzled head and glanced nervously at Beau. Father came back with his black medicine bag. Mr. Carney followed my parents into the bedroom. Mother was used to caring for sick people because she had been a nurse before she met Father. When the door to the little room opened, I could just make out a lumpy figure on the bed under a frayed pink-and-white quilt. I tried not to stare.

Once again Beau and I were left alone in the kitchen. Beau took a battered kettle off the stove and began pumping water into it. The Carneys didn't have regular faucets. Then he went outside and brought in a couple of loads of wood.

The sun was well over the horizon by now, casting a golden glow over the cornfield I had circled an hour before. From the kitchen window I thought I saw a flock of crows dotting the alder bushes around the field, but I couldn't be certain.

"Have you had many crows in your cornfield?" I asked Beau as he came in with the second load of logs.

"Some."

"Do they pull up your plants?"

"Some do, some don't," he said.

"And what do you do to the ones that do?" I asked.

"You sure like to ask a lot of questions," said Beau.

I was about to ask Beau if he'd seen our warning signs on the road when Mother returned to the kitchen and asked for the telephone book. Beau rummaged around in a drawer.

"You going to phone for some medicine from Muldoon's?"

"Well, actually," said Mother, a note of hesitation in her voice, "actually it's a little more serious than that, I'm afraid."

She put the phone book down and came over to Beau, who was standing at the kitchen sink.

"I'm calling the ambulance service in Ellbridge. The doctor thinks it would be best to take your mother to the hospital in Bangor."

"Geez! Bangor is fifty miles from here! What's wrong with her? Is she going to be all right?"

"She'll certainly be more comfortable at the hospital than she is here," said Mother.

"How long is she going to be up there?" asked Beau.

"I can't tell you that," said Mother. "We're going to make arrangements for your father to stay in a room near the hospital. He'll be able to visit her whenever he wants."

Beau stared out the window and swallowed hard. Finally he turned to Mother and took a deep breath. "She'll be comin' back here, won't she? This isn't . . ." He paused, searching for the right word. "This isn't . . . permanent, is it?"

"She certainly will be coming back!" said Mother. "Now you get those black thoughts right out of your head, Beauregard!"

51

"I guess me and Bozo is going to be here by our- selves for a while."

"Oh, no," said Mother calmly. "Bozo is going to the kennel. You are going to stay at our house."

Beau stared at her in disbelief.

"Pack up a few clothes," she continued. "We'll carry your things back to our house, and the doctor can wait with your parents for the ambulance."

"I'm staying right here, and nobody's going to make me leave," said Beau, plunking himself down on the stack of newspapers and crossing his arms defiantly. He was staring very hard out the kitchen window.

Mother didn't say anything. She walked over and gently put her hand on his shoulder. Father came out and phoned the ambulance. It would be at least an hour, he said. Then he called a doctor in Bangor and they began discussing Mrs. Carney's condition. You couldn't understand a word they said because it was all medical talk, but you got the idea that they didn't want to waste any time. After that, Mother made arrangements with the kennel.

"Where's your suitcase?" asked Mother softly.

"I ain't going," muttered Beau. "Besides, we ain't got no suitcases."

"How about a paper bag then?"

"I told you, I'm staying here," said Beau. "The bags is under the sink."

"Where are your clothes?"

52

"They're in the drawer over there," said Beau. "But I told you, Mrs. Berry, I'm planning to stay here."

"I know you want to, Beau, but you don't have any choice. We don't know how long your father will have to stay in Bangor, and your mother needs him up there to help her get well. Your father says the rest of your family lives far away."

"North Carolina," muttered Beau.

"It won't be for long. You'll have fun with the girls. Why, you've lived next door almost three months and we've hardly met."

Mother bent over the drawer and tucked some wadded-up clothing into a bag. Beau watched with a grumpy frown. On the one hand, you could tell that the last thing he wanted was to move to a strange house, but on the other hand, he realized there was no stopping my mother once she'd made up her mind.

"Think I could go in and see Ma for a minute?" said Beau, suddenly resigned. "I guess I better say good-bye to my folks."

He shoved his hands into his pockets and slouched into the bedroom. Through the half-open door I saw Mr. Carney sitting on the pink-and-white quilt holding his wife's hand. I still couldn't see Mrs. Carney's face.

"Now, Lou," said Mother, "you take this bag and run on home. I left a note for Stephanie, but she's probably wondering what's taking us so long. Beau and I will be back in an hour or so."

I turned toward the bedroom one more time.

"Now run along," said Mother. "You haven't even had any breakfast. The cereal is on the kitchen table."

I picked up the bag and walked down the driveway, past the toilet planted with flowers. It seemed unbelievable. I'd gone to the Carneys' to save our pet crow from being shot by his enemy. I was going home with a bagful of the enemy's dirty clothes. I wondered what Stephanie would think when I told her.

The sun had climbed high in the sky, although the trees still cast long morning shadows over the road. I looked back at the Carneys' and wondered what it would be like having Beau live at our house. Where would he sit at the table, and where would he sleep? Would Mother make him wash the dirt off the back of his neck?

Up ahead I could see Jennie riding her tricycle in her bathrobe in the driveway. Stephanie had the binoculars out, zeroing in on the Carneys'.

"What's going on?" she shouted, running down the road toward me, the binoculars flopping against her chest. "Why in the world did you go to the Carneys'? What's all the excitement about? Where are Mother and Father? What's in that bag?"

"Beauregard Carney's dirty clothes," I said.

"What?" said Stephanie.

"It's Beau's dirty clothes."

"Are you crazy? Are you going into the laundry business or something? And what's this 'Beau' business? Since when do we call Beauregard Carney 'Beau'?"

"That's what his father calls him," I said. I wondered how to break the news gently. "By the way, Beau is coming to live with us."

"He's coming to live at *our* house?" gasped Stephanie. "Beauregard Carney? The juvenile delinquent?"

Stephanie glared at me. For a minute I felt as if I'd done something awful.

"He's not a juvenile delinquent. It just so happens that his mother is very sick and has to go to the hospital."

I launched into the whole story. Stephanie's eyes grew wider as I slipped out the details to her one by one.

"Well!" she exclaimed. "I don't know where Mother gets these bright ideas. Beauregard Carney! A common thief! At our house! What can Mother be thinking of? I'm going to lock up my stuff right this minute."

"Stephanie, his mother is very sick. She might even d—"

"And the kids at school! What will Marty and Jody say when they hear this?" said Stephanie, wringing her hands. "We'll be eating supper with a criminal!"

I let Stephanie sound off for a few minutes longer. We'd have to share everything—the comics, the bathroom, the radio, the bikes. He would torture the animals, and smudge the piano keys, and slurp his food.

I stuffed Beau's clothes into the washing machine and poured in the soap. The machine began to hum. As I ate my Rice Krispies, I was thinking of the light dust of freckles on Beau's cheeks. And the way his hair fell across his forehead into his eyes. And the salt-sea color of his eyes.

Stephanie kept fretting as she made the rounds of the house with an empty laundry basket, putting into it everything she thought might attract a thief's attention—our piggy banks, of course, and the trophies we won at Girl Scout camp last summer, her charm bracelet, the butterfly collection, and a ton of other stuff. She locked them all in a suitcase and put the key in her pocket.

It wasn't long before the Ellbridge ambulance sped past our house on the way to the Carneys'. Fifteen minutes later it zoomed by, going the other direction.

I hadn't realized till I saw Beau standing next to my parents, as they got out of the Jeep, how tall he was—several inches taller than either of them. His hands were still jammed into his pockets, and he studied his shoelaces a lot.

Stephanie was hiding out in the house with the binoculars. But Jennie, still in the driveway in her bathrobe, came right over to Beau and held her hand out for him to shake.

"Hi, I'm Jennifer Edith Berry. I'm awful glad you came over. Know why? Now you won't try to kill our crow. You know us, so you won't shoot at him anymore. Now we're friends, I don't have to worry."

Beau's frown changed into an embarrassed smile. He looked away.

"Want to see me do some tricks on my tricycle?"

"Tricycle? Yeah, oh sure. I'd like to," he said.

Jennie began pedaling at a snail's pace down the driveway, lifting her hands off the handlebars and grinning over her shoulder.

"Wow," said Beau. "You're pretty hot on that machine, ain't you?"

"I'm a great rider," said Jennie. "Do you really steal stuff?"

Beau looked nervously toward Mother. She was busy pulling some of the Carneys' old blankets out of the Jeep and conferring with Father about what time he'd get back from Bangor, so she wasn't paying attention.

"Naah. Stealing ain't right," mumbled Beau.

"Stephanie says you do," said Jennie.

"Oh, yeah?"

"Yep. She says you took some groceries from the A&P."

I thought we'd kept the A&P a secret from Jennie, but it looked like she'd figured it out anyway.

"Oh, yeah? Who is this Stephanie anyway?"

"Stephanie Ann Berry is my big sister," she said matter-of-factly, "and Louise Emily Berry is my next biggest sister."

Beau's eyes met mine. Then we both looked away. Beau fidgeted with his belt buckle, but I knew he was warming up to Jen as she chattered away. A smile curled on his lips.

"Hey, why did you go over to the Carneys' this morning, Lou?" said Jennie, turning to me suddenly. "We never go over to the Carneys'. Not after the robbery. The robbery at the A&P."

I knelt down next to Jennie's tricycle.

"I went to the Carneys' because I was worried Beau would shoot our crow . . . by mistake. I put chicken grain down around their field for Crow to eat. That way he wouldn't bother their corn."

"So that was it," murmured Beau, half aloud.

For the first time Jennie looked worried.

"Beau won't shoot our crow now, will he? Now that he knows us?"

"No, no. Beau would never hurt our crow on purpose, Jennie. He feels the same way we do about pets."

"Beau loves animals, right?" said Jennie.

"Ask him. He'll tell you," I said, staring him right in the eye.

Beau shuffled his feet in the gravel of the driveway. Jennie looked hopefully in his direction.

"Oh, sure. I'm a real animal lover all right," he said. "I wouldn't hurt a flea! Why, that old dog Bozo is my best friend."

"Oh, Beau. I knew you would be nice. Stephanie was wrong!" A huge grin spread over Jennie's face. She beamed happily at Beau, then turned the tricycle around and set off down the driveway pedaling with all her might. She was showing off.

"This Stephanie live here?" asked Beau, not taking his eyes off Jennie and her tricycle.

Before I could answer, the screen door slammed and my older sister came out onto the steps.

"There you are, Lou. Can I borrow your Bible? I have to do the Scripture reading for Sunday school tomorrow, and I want to practice."

Beau folded his arms and leaned back against the car, looking up at her.

"Oh, hello," said Stephanie from the top step. "You'll be staying with us for a short while, I understand."

"Till my ma gets out of the hospital."

"Oh really, how nice," said Stephanie. She flipped her ponytail. "Well, excuse me, please, I must go and reread the Ten Commandments for Sunday school. . . . 'Thou shalt not steal' . . . stuff like that."

The door banged a second time. Beau whistled under his breath.

"Whew! She's something else."

Stephanie's head poked out the door. "Oh, by the way, I'm sorry to hear about your mother, Beauregard."

Then she turned on her heel and was gone.

CHAPTER FIVE

"Did you see that?" Stephanie gasped that night at dinner.

"See what?" asked Jennie.

We were seated around the table for the first time. Six people instead of five. Beau was down at the far end, between my parents.

"The butter knife!" hissed Stephanie in an undertone. "He didn't use the butter knife! What did I tell you!"

In the center of the table was a cake of soft butter, and Beau had reached over and was dragging his corn bread smoothly across the top. Big yellow globs stuck to his fingers. Beau glanced quickly at the faces around the table, drew back his hand, and wiped it on his pants.

"Disgusting," said Stephanie, wrinkling her nose the way girls do when they see something gross.

Mother glanced up. "How about some jam for your corn bread too, Beau?"

"Oh, no thanks, ma'am," said Beau nervously.

He nibbled off the corner of the bread and put it carefully on the place mat, the buttered side up. Stephanie groaned.

"Know why Stephanie is acting so awful, Beau?" Jennie hopped down from her chair and came over and leaned against Beau's arm. Mother started chewing like crazy, hurrying to swallow in order to steer to a safer topic.

"First of all you ate your bread sloppy," began my little sister. "Next you forgot to use your napkin. Then you put the bread down on the place mat instead of your plate. You're supposed to put it on your plate. Otherwise the place mats get all sticky and we can't use them again."

Jennie leaned over and examined the corner of Beau's place mat.

"Hey! Here's some macaroni and cheese glued on from last night!"

Stephanie nearly choked. Beau stared down at his plate, his hand hiding his mouth.

"Ever candled eggs before, Beau?" asked Father brightly.

"No, sir, ain't had the chance," said Beau, licking his fingers and shooting a quick glance at Stephanie out of the corner of his eye.

"Well, tomorrow I'll show you how. It's done by holding the egg up to the light to make sure the egg hasn't been fertilized." Father launched into a sci-entific explanation, and pretty soon no one was listening except Mother. Stephanie had laid on a sickly sweet smile and was dabbing at the corners of her mouth with a napkin. Suddenly Jennie reached over Beau's arm and grabbed his corn bread.

"Jennifer!" exploded Stephanie. Jenny had stuffed the whole piece of bread into her mouth at once.

"Cal-buss-bahs. You neh Cal-buss," she said, not paying Stephanie the slightest attention. Yellow crumbs sprayed out in tiny puffs all over the table. This time he couldn't help it. Beau grinned.

"Jennifer!" snapped Stephanie. "What's the matter with you? You know we don't take other people's food, and we certainly don't talk with our mouths full!"

Jennie swallowed. "I said, Calvert's. Beau needs Calvert's. That's how you get good manners and stuff, right, Lou? You do Calvert's. Then you can visit a queen."

I nodded. Calvert's was some institute in Maryland that sent out educational books to people like us living way out in the sticks. If you couldn't go to nursery school, your mother could teach you at home using one of the Calvert School's specially prepared manuals. They had a whole book on nothing but how to act polite. According to Mother, by the time you finished Calvert's you'd be ready to meet the queen herself.

After dinner Stephanie washed the dishes and Beau and I dried. Mother told Beau that he didn't have to help since he was company, but he said he always did the dishes at home, so he didn't mind.

"I'll bet you five dollars that boy has never washed a dish in his life," whispered Stephanie as she filled the sink with soapy water.

In the other room Beau was clearing the dishes onto a tray. I wondered what we could talk about, now that Jennie and Mother and Father had gone. I shouldn't have worried. As soon as Beau pushed through the kitchen door with the tray loaded with dishes, my sister started in.

"You know the one thing I can't stand? People who say 'ain't.' It sounds so common, don't you agree, Lou?" She looked pointedly at me.

I didn't know what to say. Beau was standing right next to us, fumbling in the kitchen drawer for a towel.

"Oh, I don't know," I mumbled.

"Mrs. Blaisdell, my teacher, says 'ain't' is the mark of a truly uneducated person."

Beau had found a towel and was twisting it up tight as a corkscrew. "Don't say 'ain't,' " he said, grinning stiffly. " 'Ain't' ain't in the dictionary."

"Oh, Lord," said Stephanie. She pursed her lips and began washing silverware.

"Guess what, Beau," I said. "We used to tell our mother we couldn't dry the knives because we were afraid we'd cut ourselves. And she really believed us too."

"Oh, yeah?" said Beau.

"Well, maybe *you* did, Louise. I always dried everything, knives and all," said Stephanie.

"Oh, that's because you were always so mature, Stephanie," I retorted. I tried to catch Beau's eye, but he was working over the same glass he'd picked up a minute ago.

Stephanie started out fresh.

"It's so important to save your allowance, don't you think?"

"Allowance?" I said.

"You know. Christmas money. Birthday money. Save it up. Like we do."

Stephanie and I had over forty dollars between us gathering dust in the Ellbridge National Bank.

"That way, if something comes up and you need money all of a sudden," Stephanie paused and cleared her throat. "That way you don't have to do anything . . . extreme."

I thought Beau was going to drop the glass. But he didn't. "Uh . . . where does this go?" was all he said.

I pointed to the shelf to the right of the sink.

"I hope you realize you never sterilized that glass," said Stephanie. "You're supposed to pour boiling water over the dishes before you dry them. Otherwise it spreads germs. I thought you said you did the dishes at home."

I couldn't believe it. Stephanie was acting awful.

If I were Beau, I would have wrapped the dish towel around her neck and strangled her. She couldn't leave off pestering him any more than a tongue can quit fiddling with a loose tooth.

Beau's expression hardly changed. Well, maybe it firmed up a tiny bit at the corners of the mouth. He took the kettle Stephanie handed him and poured hot water over the glasses and silverware. That was it. He didn't say another word. Stephanie turned on the radio, and we listened to the hit parade till the dishes were done. Then Beau went up to the cot Mother had made up for him in the back bedroom.

"What a sourpuss," said Stephanie after Beau left. "All he does is mope around. He hardly says one word, and he has such a gloomy look on his face."

"Well, you might at least give the kid a chance," I said.

"A chance? What do you mean, a chance? This is his opportunity to find out how really civilized people live."

"Oh, come off it, Stephanie," I said. "He's probably worried sick about his mother."

"Well, the least he could do would be to show one measly sign of improvement. The very least."

"He's not stealing anything," I said.

"He's probably waiting till we're out of the house," said Stephanie. "Don't you worry, Lou. I'm not taking any chances. I have the key to the suitcase right here." She patted her pocket.

The next day was better. After we got back from Sunday school, Father taught Beau how to candle the eggs so he'd have something to do. You held each egg in front of a light to check for dark spots and weighed them on a little scale, putting them into boxes according to size. Beau candled six dozen. Then he disappeared behind the chicken house.

At least that's where I found him an hour later, when Mother sent Jennie and me out to see if he wanted to go into town for a late afternoon ice cream at the Dairy Queen. He was perched on a stack of chicken crates tossing sticks into the air for Crowberry to catch. I was relieved. It was the first time I'd seen him play with Crow.

"Hey, Beau. Want to ride into Ellbridge and get an ice cream?" called Jennie.

He looked startled, sat up quickly, and turned his eyes away, but not before I'd seen how red they looked around the edges. I didn't know teenage boys cried. I remembered the quavering voice and faded quilt I'd run into at Beau's house the day before.

"Naw. I ain't hungry," said Beau huskily. "You go ahead."

"Oh, come on," I said. "Stephanie has sucked the juice out of the eighth commandment. She finished her church speech this morning."

"Oh, she don't bother me none. I seen worse. You go on. I'm going back over to the house to check up on things. You go on without me."

"They've got chocolate dip tops," said Jennie. "That's what I'm going to have."

Beau sighed. Then he picked up a twig and tossed it up to Crowberry. We watched the bird swerve sharply before snapping the twig in his beak.

"Hey, fella, you're pretty smart," said Beau softly. "Pretty dang smart."

Crow touched down at our feet and let Jennie tug on the stick for a minute before letting go.

"I know your mother is getting better, Beau," I said suddenly. "My father is a real good doctor."

"Yep," said Beau.

"So you don't have to worry. She'll get better. I know it."

I studied Beau's face. His hair was yellow as straw, but his eyelashes were dark. I wished he wouldn't turn away whenever I looked at him. And he was so quiet. I wondered if we would ever get him to talk.

"They've got hot fudge sundaes," said Jennie.

"What?"

"Hot fudge sundaes with whipped cream and nuts. And a cherry."

"No. You go without me," repeated Beau, climbing down off the crates. "I got to be seeing after our place like I told Pa."

"Well, I'll see you later then," I said. "But I know she'll get well."

"Yep," said Beau. "She better."

I tossed one last handful of hay into the air for

Crowberry. Then I took Jennie by the hand and we walked slowly back toward the house.

"Beau feels sad because his mother might die, right, Louise?"

I nodded.

"But she's not going to, right?"

"Right," I said.

"How do you know she's not going to die?"

"I just know it," I said suddenly. "Now quit asking me questions. I can't wait for that chocolate dip top."

"Me too," said Jennie. Her hand was warm and sticky in mine.

"I was polite, wasn't I, Louise?"

"What do you mean?"

"I didn't tell Beau that his mother might die. Even though I thought she might."

"You did exactly right to keep it a secret," I said.

"I know," said Jennie. "Guess what." She stopped and looked up at me with a smile. "You can come with me if you want to."

"Come with you to the ice cream place? I *am* coming with you, silly."

"No, Louise, you can come with me," she repeated, "when we go to visit that queen."

CHAPTER SIX

"**G**uess what!" shouted Stephanie over the roar of the lawn mower the next day as I was cutting the grass. She shook me excitedly, a smile of satisfaction lighting up her face. "Beauregard is torturing the kittens!"

She held up one of Redhead's babies. Its eyes were open, but it was still pretty wobbly on its feet. I switched off the motor.

"How do you know?"

"Look at his tail! This kitten's tail looks red and chewed up on the end. And there are two more just like it."

I had to admit, there was a tiny drop of dried blood caked in the kitten's fur at the tip of his tail.

"I'll bet Beauregard is flinging them around when we aren't looking. Let's tell Mother!"

"Have you seen him do it?" I asked.

"Well, not exactly. But I wouldn't put it past him."

As my sister told her about the kittens, Mother smiled mysteriously.

"Stephanie, get some milk and put it out on the lawn. Louise, you get the kittens. Then both of you come into the house."

We watched from the kitchen window as the furry bodies of Redhead's six kittens crowded around the saucer of milk.

"Why are we doing this? Are we setting a trap for Beauregard or something?" asked Stephanie.

"Not for Beau." Mother smiled.

Moments later the familiar wings flapped overhead and Crowberry settled down behind the tiniest kitten. He clamped his beak shut on its tail and slowly pulled it backward. Then he wormed his way into the open spot to get a drink.

Stephanie screwed her face into a frown. "Well, it *could* have been Beauregard," she mumbled. "You never know."

Mother put both arms on my sister's shoulders and looked her full in the face. Stephanie hung her head. "Stephanie, I could give you a very long lecture," said Mother, "but I'm not going to because I think you know what I'd say."

Stephanie was silent.

"What would I say?" asked Mother.

Stephanie's eyes got watery and her mouth quivered.

"What would I say, Lou?" said Mother, turning to me.

"Don't blame people for stuff they didn't do."

"Yes?"

I couldn't think of anything else at the moment. And if I did, I couldn't say it because Stephanie would brain me later.

"I think you girls understand. I want you to treat Beau like a member of the family. He's having a hard time getting used to being away from home. Especially not knowing about his mother. So we've got to try extra hard to give him a good time while he's here."

"But Mother!" wailed Stephanie. "He's not like us!"

"You haven't given him a chance to show what he *is* like," said Mother softly. "I want to see you both making a special effort to include him in what you're doing. Marbles or whatever. None of this Bible and table manners business, please."

"Mother, you promised, no lecture," said Stephanie. She blew her nose and sniffed. "We'll think of something. Don't worry."

The telephone rang and Mother hurried off to answer it.

"What could we do?" I said. "Sleep out in a tent behind the barn?"

"Are you kidding?" said Stephanie.

"How about setting up a roadside stand? We could sell something."

"What, for instance?"

"We could go clamming and sell the clams."

"Too smelly," said Stephanie.

We listened to Mother's voice on the telephone. It was Dr. Butler calling. When she came back, she told us Dr. Butler's aunt was visiting from Palm Springs and they were going to drop by and see us. The thought of Dr. Butler being young enough to have an aunt seemed pretty strange.

"Miss Eleanor Fundenburg is her name. You will have to be on your best behavior. She's not used to children."

"Is she used to crows?" asked Jennie.

"I'm *sure* she's not used to crows!" Mother laughed. "Now, girls, ask Beau to help you set up some lawn chairs and the picnic table on the back lawn. That's something you can all do together."

Beau was shooting stones at spider webs in the barn when we found him. When everything was finally set up, Stephanie announced, "I'm going to wash up, brush my hair, and clean my fingernails. Dirty fingernails are disgusting, don't you think, Lou?"

It was sure going to take a miracle to make Stephanie quit bugging Beau. He jammed his hands into his pockets and headed into the house.

"That kid is such a pain," muttered Stephanie.

At three thirty Dr. Butler's Packard pulled into the driveway. Father was out on a house call, Jennie was still having her nap, and Beau was nowhere in sight. Mother shooed Stephanie and me away from the window, but not before we had caught a glimpse of Aunt Eleanor. She was adjusting her flowered hat in the rearview mirror and straightening her white gloves. Dr. Butler rushed to open the car door. We smoothed down our dresses and hurried out to greet the guests.

With her mane of blond hair, Aunt Eleanor looked like an aging movie star. She had a ton of makeup on and enough jewelry to fill a pirate's treasure chest. As soon as she stepped out of the car, I had her pegged for one of those phony summer people.

"How do you do, Mrs. Berry. What a quaint little farm you have! It's a shame I don't get here more often, I travel so much you know. Oh, Teddy," she called to Dr. Butler. "Bring my wrap, will you, darling? It's a little chilly."

Dr. Butler hustled to the car.

I was trying to get used to the idea of anyone calling old Dr. Butler "Teddy" when I saw out of the corner of my eye Aunt Eleanor making straight for me.

"Say something," Stephanie hissed behind me. "Something pleasant!"

I can never think of anything to say around grown-ups. In fact I had been concentrating on Aunt Eleanor's shoes, which were white high heels with open toes through which you could see bright red toenail polish.

"Hi," I said. "I like your shoes."

"Ninny!" whispered Stephanie.

"What did you say, dear?" asked Aunt Eleanor.

My sister pushed in front of me and held out her hand.

"How do you do, Miss Fundenburg. I'm Stephanie, and this is my sister Louise. We're so glad you could come. It's a lovely day today, isn't it?"

Dr. Butler returned with Aunt Eleanor's fur. It was one of those awful foxy ones with the heads still on.

Aunt Eleanor adjusted the fur piece over her shoulders and fixed her pearl necklace, its shiny clasp dead center at the back of her neck. Just then Beau came around the corner of the house.

"And whom have we here?" said Aunt Eleanor.

Mother introduced Beau. It looked to me like he'd combed his hair. And he actually held out his hand.

"You look like a nice young man," said Aunt Eleanor. "And what are you doing to keep busy this summer?"

"Well," said Beau, fishing around for something to say, "I guess I been messing around a lot."

"Messing around?" Aunt Eleanor wrinkled her nose, put on her sunglasses, and studied Beau like

75

a germ under a microscope. I wondered if Dr. Butler had told her about his problems at the A&P.

"Children of today have altogether too much free time, don't you agree, Mrs. Berry?"

"Well, Beau has been a big help with the eggs," said Mother.

"I try to stay busy with my Girl Scout badges," piped up Stephanie. "I just got my First Class."

"Did you, dear? That's nice," said Aunt Eleanor. "You have such lovely children, Mrs. Berry." Beau began rubbing his chin and edging toward the house. In a moment he was gone.

"Well, girls, how's the crow?" said Dr. Butler, suddenly breaking into the conversation.

I launched into the story of the Sunday school picnic.

"Teddy told me about your little pet," interrupted Aunt Eleanor. "I suppose it is a wonderful thing for children. But I must confess, I'm quite nervous in the presence of animals. Such unpredictable creatures. And dirty, too. I don't know how Teddy stands it. I prefer the more civilized pleasures."

"I'm sure you're not alone," said Mother.

"If there's one thing I can't stand, it's dirt," continued Aunt Eleanor. "I simply abhor it. A bad habit I picked up from my travels, I suppose."

"Let's have our tea in the backyard," said Mother, signaling for us to stay put. "I want to hear all about your trip to Paris." She had Aunt Eleanor's number. Kids were best tucked out of sight.

"Well!" exclaimed Stephanie, when they were safely out of hearing. "If I see one more lazy, rotten, good-for-nothing child, I shall go right out of my mind!"

She thrust out her chin and poked me in the chest, mimicking Aunt Eleanor's snooty tone.

"That spot of dirt behind your left ear. Totally uncalled for!"

"My darling," I said, trying not to giggle. "I'm so offended by that dog hair on your sock, I simply can't move."

Stephanie snickered. "No, no. It's that moldy Cheerio stuck on your cheek!"

"It's that disgusting splat of baked beans on your sleeve!"

"It's that meatball squished behind your glasses!"

"It's that tomato stain on your collar!"

"No, no, my precious," wailed Stephanie, "it's that wad of bubble gum on your forehead!"

We dissolved in gales of laughter.

All of a sudden Beau stuck his head out the door. He must have been listening the whole time, because he said with a twinkle in his eye, "Ladies, it's them scummy, fly-spotted elbows!"

Stephanie whirled around in amazement. I thought her eyes would pop right out of her skull.

"What did you say?"

"He said, 'them scummy, fly-spotted elbows.' "
I laughed.

I knew Beau was just trying to be friendly. I smiled at him.

"It's rude to eavesdrop," Stephanie said, frowning suddenly. Her voice was as cold as ice, and her eyes matched. "It's really terribly rude. By the way, 'them elbows' is bad grammar."

Beau straightened his shoulders and the smile faded from his face. Stephanie had done it again. I don't know what would have happened if Mother hadn't called her to bring the tea stuff out to the backyard just then.

When she was gone I said to Beau, "Don't mind Stephanie. She's always like that. 'Fly-spotted elbows'? What a scream."

I smiled at Beau again. He looked at me soberly.

"Hey," I said, "we can get a muffin out of this deal at least. Come on."

Without a word Beau followed me to the backyard. I knew what was coming because I'd seen the white linen napkins, spotless china teacups, and tiny date muffins on Mother's best silver tray in the kitchen.

"Oh, thank you so much," Aunt Eleanor was saying as Stephanie put the tray down carefully in front of her. "What was your name again, dear?"

"Stephanie," said my sister. "I'm twelve going on—"

"Oh, Mrs. Berry, could I trouble you to hand me one of those napkins? There seems to be a trace of dust on this chair," said Aunt Eleanor. "I hope you don't mind, my dear."

She turned around and was just starting to spread the napkin on the seat when Mother's eyes opened wide and her mouth fell open in horror.

"Eleanor! Duck! Duck! Get down!"

Crowberry touched down on Aunt Eleanor's shoulder and pulled with all his might on the shiny clasp of her necklace. Aunt Eleanor screamed. Her hat flew off and she waved her arms wildly in the air. You'd have thought she'd been attacked by a swarm of bees.

Beau jumped forward and swatted Crow away with Aunt Eleanor's hat. The crow dropped to the ground and was eyeing the red toenail polish with interest when Beau nabbed him from behind. It looked to me as if he was trying not to laugh.

"Hey!" exclaimed Beau suddenly. "Crowberry is covered with ants!"

It was true! A swarm of ants was crawling all over Crow, into his eyes and beak and under his feathers.

"Ants! Oh, no!" screamed Aunt Eleanor, beating her hair and fur like a madwoman.

"Ants?" chimed in Dr. Butler. "Fascinating. You know I've read about 'anting' in the ornithological literature, but I've never seen it firsthand. Let's have a look."

"Oh, dear me, dear me!" Aunt Eleanor rolled her eyes and fanned herself like crazy with her hat.

"It has to do with the formic acid found naturally in some ants." Dr. Butler mumbled about vesicatory properties as he examined the skin underneath Crowberry's feathers. Aunt Eleanor was flushed red clear through all three layers of makeup and seemed about ready to collapse.

"I am so terribly sorry, Eleanor," said Mother, wringing her hands. "That crow is totally out of control. Let's go to the kitchen and get a glass of cold water."

"Are you all right, Eleanor?" asked Dr. Butler finally. "Why don't you all go back into the house. I have some insect powder in my bag. A most interesting phenomenon."

I stood and stared at Crowberry, not knowing whether to laugh or cry.

"Too bad he didn't do his business on her fur!" whispered Stephanie, grinning mischievously as we watched Aunt Eleanor follow Mother into the house.

I wandered over to the car. Beau held Crow firmly while Dr. Butler sprinkled white powder under his wings and on his back and tail feathers.

"There, fellow, you're all set," said the veterinarian, giving him a couple of pats, sending a cloud of white insecticide into the air. Crowberry took off for a nearby pine tree.

"Guess I'd better check Aunt Eleanor for ants

next," said Dr. Butler with a wink, flourishing the can of insecticide in the air.

The rest of the afternoon passed slowly. Beau took an ax out behind the barn and split wood. Stephanie collected Jennie from her nap. Father returned from his house call. As soon as I told him what had happened, he hurried into the house. Father was used to tight situations. In a few minutes we heard Aunt Eleanor laughing, and before long things seemed to be back to normal.

I kept a sharp lookout for Crowberry. He was cruising back and forth between the house and barn. Finally, he plunked down on the hood of Dr. Butler's Packard and began to pull off one of the windshield wipers.

"Crow!" I moaned, racing over to the car. "You little rascal! You're asking for trouble!"

I pried him away from the windshield wiper and stood guard over the car until Aunt Eleanor and Dr. Butler came out of the house. The grown-ups all looked happy.

"Are you sure you won't come out and let me show you the chickens?" said Father with a wicked smile.

"Another day," said Aunt Eleanor. Glancing nervously overhead, she sprinted to the car. "Do say thank you to that nice boy who rescued me!" she called from the car. Dr. Butler revved up the motor and they were off.

That night, Stephanie found a note on her pillow. Mother didn't give lectures, but she left notes. Stephanie read it, and then handed it over to me and climbed into bed. It said:

Dearest Stephanie,
Here are some ideas to think about. I found them in one of my books. Famous people first thought of them, but I will pass them on to you.
"Look for good, not evil, in people."
"The art of being wise is the art of knowing what to overlook."
"It is not enough to do good. You must do it in the right way."
Your parents love you very much.
X X X X X   Mother

I put the note on the nightstand and turned out the light. The house was quiet. Outside in the velvety darkness a full moon was rising behind the mountains. Crickets were chirping, and moths batted against the screen.

I thought of Aunt Eleanor throwing a fit because of Crow, and Beau's mother lying alone in her hospital bed in Bangor, and Mother copying from her book of quotations in the careful, spidery handwriting I knew so well.

But mostly I thought about Beau. I liked the way he catered to Jennie, and how he helped out with the eggs and the wood, and the joke he made up listening to Stephanie and me. His stepping right in and rescuing Aunt Eleanor was wonderful. I was glad he was at our house. The kid had real possibilities.

CHAPTER SEVEN

"I've got an idea," said Stephanie the next day. "Let's have a circus!"

"What kind of a circus?" I said.

"A circus with lots of different acts. You know, like animals, stunts, magic, a sideshow, a master of ceremonies, music, beautiful ladies . . ."

Stephanie paused to catch her breath. "And popcorn, soda pop, clowns, tickets, posters, tents, favors, decorations—"

"Hey, we can't do all that, just the four of us," I interrupted.

"Sure we can," said Stephanie confidently. "We can keep switching in and out of our costumes. Of course, I'll be the master of ceremonies and the beautiful trapeze artist. You can do the magic tricks and the clown act, and Jennie can sell the tickets and popcorn and stuff. Now what about Beauregard?" She cocked her head to one side. "He could do the freak section at the side show—"

"Stephanie! That's not fair!"

"You're right," said Stephanie. "He'll be in charge of the animal acts. He can figure out something for Micky and Crowberry and the kittens, maybe the chickens even. Let's go tell him the plan."

"Don't you think we should ask him if he wants to do it first?"

"Ask him?" said Stephanie.

"Yes," I said. "Not everyone likes to be in circuses, you know."

"He'll want to do it. Don't worry," said Stephanie.

I stretched out under the tree in the front yard and tried to think of magic tricks I knew. The grass was warm against my back, and big puffy clouds scudded across the sky.

Crow watched them from his perch on the roof. The ants were gone. I was glad he was safe. Beau had been at our house for only three days, but already I sensed that he was getting attached to our pet and would never try to shoot him. He'd let him land on his shoulder and tug at his shoelaces just like the rest of us.

Father had talked to the doctors at Bangor Hospital, and it looked like Beau's mother would be all right. She'd probably be in the hospital for the rest of the week. Beau's eyes glistened when Mother told him the good news.

I closed my eyes. Stephanie was calling Beau and Jennie. The wind rustled in the leaves overhead, and a blue jay was crying out in the distance. You could tell Beau was trying hard to fit in. He played crazy eights with Jennie and let her win. He hung up his towel in the bathroom and didn't hog the comics. In fact, he didn't even want to look at them. I figured the Carneys didn't subscribe, so he didn't have to stay caught up.

But he still wouldn't talk much. In fact, the only one he really talked to was Jennie.

"Hey, Beauregard, how'd you like to earn some money?" began Stephanie when she'd finally rounded everyone up.

"Doing what?" he asked.

"Being in a circus," said Stephanie. "We'll ask kids from school, sell tickets, and split the money four ways. Don't worry. I'll be in charge."

"Elephants and tigers and all them things?" asked Beau doubtfully.

"Hey, that's a good idea. I don't see why not." said Stephanie. "Stuffed, of course. Now, you're responsible for the animal acts," she continued. Beau nodded.

During the next couple of days we talked over our plans and parceled out the jobs. Before long Stephanie had everything organized. One day she even admitted to me, "You know, Lou, I didn't think Beauregard would go for this circus stuff. But he's catching on real fast."

She got on the telephone and invited some town kids for the following Saturday. About twenty people said they could come. Then she practiced on the swings to figure out some unusual new ways of hanging from the trapeze. Jennie made red-and-green squiggles on little pieces of construction paper for the tickets.

I thumbed through a book of magic tricks for ideas. There was a good one using a hard-boiled egg. You put the egg in a glass of water that has been mixed up with a lot of salt, and miraculously, it floats. Next I figured out how to tie a scarf so that when you untied it, it fell apart like magic. For the clown act I was going to glue some cups and saucers to a tray and pretend to spill them, tripping over my floppy clown feet.

"I wonder how Beauregard is coming with the animal act?"

It was dress rehearsal, and Stephanie was wearing her bathing suit with a gauzy pink sash around her head.

Suddenly Beau appeared around the corner of the barn with Micky, our little brown mutt, in tow.

"I'm ready," he said.

"What are you going to do? Need some dress-up clothes for Micky?"

"Nope," said Beau.

"Want me to write out your lines for you?"

"Nope, don't need 'em," said Beau.

"How about the wagon? Want to hitch Micky up to it and have him pull the kittens around?"

"I got other plans for Micky," said Beau.

Stephanie put her hands on her hips and glared.

"Well, can we watch you practice your act ahead of time? After all, we're all in this together. I have to make sure what you're doing is appropriate."

"Oh, it'll be appropriate all right."

"But what'll I put in the program? How will I announce your act?"

Beau mumbled something about doing his own announcing. He wasn't going to budge one inch, and Stephanie was fuming.

"Well, if that's how you feel about it." She shrugged, tossing the pink sash over her shoulder. "Come on, Lou. We know when we're not wanted."

For a moment I hesitated. Micky thumped his tail against Beau's blue jeans.

"Are you coming or aren't you?" repeated Stephanie.

I stole a glance at Beau's face. A smile was playing over his lips, and for a split second he shot an eye-twinkling grin in my direction. I felt happy as a clam.

"Yes, I'm coming," I said. The power struggle was on between Stephanie and Beau, but I knew I'd be sitting on the sidelines.

"What's the matter with you, dummy?" Stephanie fairly screamed into my ear when we were out of earshot. "Don't you realize what a bad influence he is?"

"Bad influence?" I said happily. "I don't think he's a bad influence. I think he's fun."

"You know what I think? I think you're getting entirely too fond of Beauregard Carney. That's what I think." She paused for effect. "Peewee!"

I kept my mouth shut. What Stephanie said was true, I knew it. She was counting the days till Beau would be leaving, but I was hoping they'd keep his mother a little longer at the hospital. I guess I was wishing that he was the brother I'd never had. I didn't want him to go.

Sisters are nice. I loved Jennie's funny ideas, the time she tried to sell pinecones at the homemade stand when there were about fifty million lying by the roadside for anybody to pick up. And in spite of the way she tried to run my life all the time, it was nice having an older sister like Stephanie, who tried to steer me in the right direction, paved the way for me in school, and warned me what things were going to be like ahead of time.

But Beau made things seem different. He was unlike any kid I'd ever met. At first I thought there was something sad and mysterious about him. But now I was beginning to see another side, one that was silly and fun. And besides, he was a boy. And we didn't know very many boys, at least not very well.

It was driving Stephanie nuts that he wouldn't let her in on his circus plans. He'd added Jennie to his act, and she was thrilled. Every morning they took Crow and Micky out behind the barn to practice.

"You been learning your lines like I told you to?"

"Oh, yes," Jennie beamed. "Announcing the Grand Master of the—"

"Shhhh! Hey, don't tell 'em. It's our secret!"

"Come on, Beau, won't you give us a hint?" pleaded Stephanie.

"You'll find out, come Saturday." He shrugged in an offhand way, which drove Stephanie berserk.

To make the circus last longer, we decided to have a sideshow. Before the circus began, the audience would have half an hour to see the "weird and wonderful attractions from all over the globe" set up in the garage. Jennie was the tattooed lady. Father was going to draw pictures of wyandotte chickens all over her arms and legs. Stephanie was to wear a hula skirt made out of strips of newspaper over her bathing suit as the exotic dancer from the tropics. I was bundled up with pillows to be a combination fat lady and fortune teller.

Beau was the talking head. He had to sit inside a huge cardboard box with a hole cut in the top for his head, so you couldn't see his neck, and say stuff when money was put in the slot. Beau wanted to charge five cents for each speech, but Stephanie said that was too high, a penny apiece was fine. They compromised at two cents.

"I've got a pain in my heart!" exclaimed Jennie as the clock inched toward two o'clock the day of the circus.

"That's called stage fright." Stephanie smeared blue-gray blobs of eyeshadow over Jennie's eyes. "It's perfectly natural."

"What do I tell them when they ask for their fortunes?" I asked.

It was stifling under the fat-lady padding.

"Make up something," said Stephanie, applying bright-red lipstick to Jennie's lips. "Go like this, Jen." She pulled her lips into a tight *O* over her teeth. "How about"—she lowered her voice dramatically— "beware of number seven."

"Tell all of them beware of seven?"

"Of course not, silly. Tell some of them beware of sixes or horses or Mondays or pickles," said Stephanie. "Tell them to count the white nicks on their fingernails to see how many children they'll have."

I was just counting the nicks on my fingernails when Mother poked her head in the door to announce the first arrivals. We rushed to our stations in the garage for the sideshow.

The next hour whizzed by in a blur. Carloads of our friends arrived—mothers and fathers, little brothers and sisters. Father churned out popcorn and Mother poured lemonade. The four of us kids waited nervously for the sideshow to begin. Marty and Jody were the first to peek through the garage door.

"Oh, how cute!" they said, spotting Jennie's tattoos. Stephanie did her hula dance, rolling her eyes and pretending not to notice that her best friends were laughing three feet away. I rubbed my crystal ball and told Marty to beware of twelves and Jody to beware of frogs. Then they approached the talking head.

"Oh, let's see what it says," said Marty, giggling nervously as she fumbled in her pocket for pennies and shoved the money through the slot.

"Nice to see you, ladies!" said the head.

Beau had white makeup plastered all over his face, red smudges around his eyes, and a white bathing cap completely covering his yellow hair. A green glass saltshaker protruded like an extra brain from the top of his head. I was amazed. His voice didn't sound nervous at all.

"And now for my latest riddle." The talking head cleared his throat.

> *"What I caught I left behind,*
> *What I brought I didn't find.*
> *What was the catch?"*

Marty and Jody gawked in astonishment at Beau's head.

"What did it say?" Jody asked.

"Double your money back for the right answer," droned the head. His voice slowed like a run-down record player. "Two . . . more . . . cents . . . please."

Stephanie stopped doing the hula act and opened her mouth to say something when Jody pulled two more cents out of her purse.

"Repeat famous riddle," said the talking head. "Riddle told in time of ancient Greeks. Said by man returning from a long journey. What did he catch?"

I'd heard the riddle before. It was one of the tricks Father used to make kids forget they were going to get a shot.

> *"What I caught I left behind,*
> *What I brought, I didn't find.*
> *What was the catch?"*

"Fish?" guessed Marty.

"Wrong," droned the talking head. "Two cents, please."

"A ball?" asked Jody.

"Wrong. Try again," said the head. "Two cents please."

The girls spent about ten cents each before finally giving up. Then they raced to tell the other kids, and before long the garage was crowded, everyone jockeying for position around the talking head, trying to guess the answer to the riddle.

"A cold?" Dr. Butler asked. Mother had invited

him and Aunt Eleanor in spite of Crow. "You caught a cold?"

"Sorry, good guess. Wrong. Two cents please."

Dr. Butler forked over two pennies. I looked over at Stephanie. She'd forgotten about her hula act. She was chewing on the crepe-paper lei and frowning.

"Time's up," said the talking head. "Last chance before correct answer."

He repeated the riddle one last time.

> *"What I caught I left behind,*
> *What I brought I didn't find.*

Tattooed Lady . . . will . . . give . . . answer."

Everyone turned to look at Jennie, who was jumping up and down, quivering with excitement.

"LICE!" she screamed. "The answer is lice!"

At first there was dead silence. Then everybody groaned.

Of course it was lice. If you catch them, you may leave them behind for other people. And their little white eggs are so tiny that they are difficult to find, growing at the base of the hair. I knew what they looked like because kids had them at Girl Scout camp last summer.

"Talking Head thanks you for attention. Please . . . take your seat for the circus. Talking Head thanks you for your attention. Please take . . . your . . . seat. . . ." Beau closed his eyes and stopped talking.

"He's cute, isn't he," Jody whispered to Marty

as they filed out. "I can't believe he's really a thief."

The rest of the circus went off pretty much as planned. Stephanie announced the magic act and I did the egg trick and a couple of others. Then I changed into my clown outfit while she performed her trapeze stunts. Everybody clapped politely. The audience fanned themselves with their programs. Finally it was time for the animal act.

Jennie and Beau disappeared into the house. Soon Micky came bounding out, dressed in old clothes from the costume box.

"Hey, he used one of my ideas after all!" whispered Stephanie.

A hush settled over the audience. Jennie placed a wooden box in the center of the backyard, climbed up, and glanced shyly at the audience.

"Go ahead, Jen!" called Beau. "You can do it!"

"I forgot what I'm supposed to say," said Jennie, giggling nervously behind her fingers.

"You remember. 'Announcing the . . .' "

"Oh, yeah," said Jennie. "Now I remember."

A titter rippled through the crowd. It didn't seem like a particularly fantastic beginning. Stephanie did her exaggerated-sigh act.

"Announcing the world-famous animal trainer from Lawrence, Maine! Master Beauregard Carney, the Great!"

Beau flipped the switch on the record player, and circus music blared out the window. Reaching into his bag, he pulled a wig of long flowing black hair over his head, buckled on a gaudy gold belt, and flung Mother's red Christmas tablecloth over his shoulders for a cape.

"Besides coming to my rescue, that fine young man is a marvelous actor," I heard Aunt Eleanor whisper to Dr. Butler.

Beau rolled his eyes, cracked his whip, and glared at the audience from under a fringe of black hair as Jennie retreated behind a large screen.

"What's that girl doing behind there?" the two-year-old behind me asked his mother.

"Wait a minute, dear. You'll see."

"Now the Magnificent Beauregard will tame the terrible beasts!" yelled Jennie.

She removed the screen, and there were Redhead's six kittens perched helplessly on top of milk cartons just like lions cowering before their tamer at a real circus. The kittens had no idea what was going on. Two hopped off their stands and Jennie had to put them back up. Beau strode back and forth, smacking the whip into the ground, shouting commands. The audience hissed and booed in a good-natured way. The mother behind me tried to explain to her child what was so funny.

"Ladies and gentlemen!" continued Jennie, "for his next trick, Beau the Great will show us that famous creature of blackness, Mr. Crowberry!"

Beau burst out of the house with Crow on his

shoulder. Aunt Eleanor stiffened in her seat, and Dr. Butler reached over and patted her on the knee.

"First, I will show you the strange friendship of bird and dog," boomed Beau. "Watch carefully. You may never see this again!"

Beau carefully transferred the crow to Micky's back. Tail between his legs, Micky took eight or ten frightened steps before rushing for the woods. The audience responded with a burst of cheers and whistles. Miraculously, Crow returned to Beau.

"That crow is pretty smart. Can we get one, Mom?" said the little boy behind me.

"Shhhhh," said his mother.

"And now for a sight you'll remember your whole long life. A real live whirlybird!" Jennie had finally warmed up to her role.

Beau uncoiled a rope from his pocket and coaxed Crowberry to take one end in his mouth. Then he gently lifted him a foot off the ground, Crow hanging like a dead weight from the end of the rope. He began to twirl around slowly so that the crow swung in an ever broader circle, clinging to the rope for dear life with his beak. After a few turns Crow lost interest and took off for his pine tree.

"So now what are you going to do, Beauregard?" yelled one of the boys in the front row. "You're stuck! The star of the show flew the coop!"

"Silence, silence," said Beau raising his arms to calm the audience. "I have amazing powers of com-

97

munication. Naturally, the only reason that bird flew away was, I ordered him to leave us. He followed my command."

"Oh, sure!" laughed the boy.

Beau pointed to the pine tree. "Stay up there, Crowberry! I command you!"

Fortunately, Crow stayed stone still in the tree. The audience groaned.

"Okay," said Beau. "To prove to you, once and for all, my power over the minds of birds, I will now attempt to bring these chickens under my complete control."

Beau gestured toward the chicken yard not far away, where the wyandottes were peacefully pecking away at bugs in the dirt.

"Bugle, please!"

Jennie handed Father's old Boy Scout bugle to Beau.

"What's he going to do, Mommy?"

"He says he's going to make the chickens do what he wants them to," whispered the mother.

"Drum roll," said Beau.

Jennie played a rat-a-tat-tat on our toy drum.

"Chickens, I command you, get out of my sight this instant!"

Ta-ta-ta-taa! Ta-ta-ta-taa! Beau sounded a tattoo on the bugle.

Like children streaming to the schoolhouse door when they hear the bell, the chickens hightailed it for the chicken house as fast as their little legs would carry them. From all over the chicken yard, they ran for their lives, kicking up little clouds of dust behind them like puffs of steam behind a locomotive. It was another old trick of Father's, scaring the chickens into the chicken coop with the bugle. The audience loved it.

"Those chickens are goofy!" exclaimed the little boy. "How did Beauregard do it, Mommy?"

I couldn't hear her answer because everyone was clapping and laughing and throwing their balled-up programs into the air. They were punching each other and blatting on fake bugles like a bunch of blathering lunatics ready for the nuthouse. The animal act was over.

"That Beauregard is a riot," said Marty. "What grade is he in?"

The grown-ups started picking up the trash, chuckling as they remembered shows they'd given as children. A few got out their cameras. Beau was surrounded by a knot of jumpy little boys. He looked happier than I'd ever seen him, holding the kids at arm's length with one hand and the bugle high in the air with the other, lining them up to take turns.

Suddenly I saw something that made my blood freeze. It was like summer turning into winter in two seconds flat.

CHAPTER EIGHT

r. Muldoon pulled his shiny black Chevrolet into the driveway. It was polished clear as a mirror. He'd come to pick up Jody, his niece.

"Is the party over yet?" he called, rolling down his window.

"Please, Uncle Pat," begged Jody. "Can't I stay just a few minutes longer? They're just serving the cake and ice cream. Please!"

Mr. Muldoon eased out of the car, tucking in his shirt and slicking back his hair. His neck was thick as a roll of baloney and his face was flushed. I remembered the last time I'd seen him at the store. What if he recognized Beau? I couldn't take any chances. Mother came over to greet him with the tray of cake and ice cream cups. She hoped he hadn't missed today's baseball game on account of the party.

I wormed my way through the crowd around Beau and tugged on his shirt. I was still wearing my clown costume, though Beau had slipped off his wig and cape. Out of the corner of my eye I could see Mr.

Muldoon peeling the wrapper off his cupcake.

"Beau!" I whispered. "You better disappear fast!"

"What?" said Beau.

I nodded toward Mother and Mr. Muldoon.

"It's Mr. Muldoon. You know. The drugstore! The magazines, remember? You better get out of here! Quick!"

Beau looked at me long and hard. He seemed to be asking a question, trying to make a connection between Mr. Muldoon and me, the kid from next door standing there dressed in a clown suit.

"Hurry! Go hide in the hayloft," I said. Mr. Muldoon was looking in our direction. "I'll tell you when it's safe to come out."

A shadow crossed Beau's face. He fixed his lips in a grim line, then turned and darted across the lawn.

Mr. Muldoon was nibbling his ice cream. He had a big head and a big mouth, and the little wooden ice cream spoon looked ridiculous in his hand.

"Mr. Muldoon says he hasn't seen you in the store much lately, Lou."

Mother was busy with the refreshments and needed somebody to make small talk with Jody's uncle. I wanted to fade out of sight.

"How are you doing, Lou?" said Mr. Muldoon, holding out a meaty hand. "You was the one that was in my store that day the kid run off with the magazines, right?"

101

"Yep. That was me," I said.

Mr. Muldoon's fingers were still sticky from frosting.

"You sure can't trust kids today," said Mr. Muldoon.

"You sure can't," I said.

"Yourself excepted, of course."

Mr. Muldoon licked a crumb off his finger. Then he told me how he caught the kids who soaped his store window last Halloween, and after that he lit into the ones who carved four-letter words in his front step and ripped up the awning out front. After what seemed like an age, Father came over and I managed to slip away. I waited around some more, until Mr. Muldoon and Jody finally left. Then I raced across the road to the barn.

"Beau! The coast is clear. They've gone!"

I scrambled up the hay bales to the top of the barn, where Beau was hiding. His knees were drawn up under his chin and he was twirling a piece of straw around his finger. The barn was fragrant with new-mown hay, and the barn swallows were darting in and out. Their babies had long since left the mud-ball nests under the eaves.

"So, how did you know about Muldoon's?" said Beau, tossing the straw down over the edge of the bales of hay, watching it as it fell through the dusty shafts of sunlight streaming in through the barn window.

"I saw you do it," I said.

Beau looked at me intently.

"You saw me at Muldoon's Drug Store?"

"Stealing the magazines, and the candy, and nail polish. Yes, I saw you," I said. "I was behind the card rack."

"The one that tipped over, you mean?"

"The one that I accidentally on purpose kicked over," I said.

"You kicked it over?" he said.

I nodded.

Beau frowned. "How come you didn't turn me in?"

"I don't know. Maybe it had something to do with your ankles."

"My ankles?"

"Yeah, your ankles. I never turn in people with knobby ankles."

Beau looked at me gratefully. Then we both burst out laughing.

"Thanks, Lou," he said. Then he leaned back against the barn wall. It was covered with cobwebs. "After I got caught at the A&P, the police told me they'd send me away if it happened again. Some detention place for kids downstate."

"Have you shoplifted stuff before, Beau?" I'd been wondering about this ever since he came.

"Some. Yes. Probably five or six times."

"Why do you do it?"

Beau tossed a piece of baling twine down to the floor below.

"It's hard to explain," he began. "When I see Ma and Pa . . . we don't have—" He broke off mid sentence.

"Have what?" I said. Beau didn't answer.

"Have what?" I repeated.

"It's so hard to talk about this stuff," said Beau.

Far away we could hear someone playing reveille on the bugle. We sat there pulling hay out of the bales and chucking it down over the edge. When Beau finally started talking, it was almost as if I wasn't even there. His voice was so low, I had to lean forward to hear him.

"We been moving ever since I can remember," said Beau. "It seems like we barely get settled down someplace when Pa gets restless and decides it's time to be on the road again. 'I hear great things about Maine, Lillian,' Pa says. 'We sure can't pass up an opportunity like this.'

"He plumb forgets he's heard great things about Altoona and Springfield and Meeker and Danbury and Decatur, and a million other places we been before that. And before you know it, we're on the road again. Driving around to places I ain't ever heard of with everything we own in the back of the pickup, checking in at the town hall in some podunk town, asking for some two-bit job to tide us over till Pa gets something permanent."

I remembered the first time I'd seen Beau and his father riding along Main Street in the rusty red pickup. As I listened, I peeled the withered seeds from a stalk of timothy grass and made a tiny yellow pile on my shoe.

"Ma, she used to raise a stink, put her foot down, say that if Pa moved us again it would be over her dead body," said Beau. "But for the past couple of years she's been slowing down a bit. Now she don't have much energy, and just goes along with Pa's plans. All the time, she's getting more tired and run-down. She can't hardly leave her bed without help. And Pa is so cheerful, like a kid almost. He don't see what's happening. Optimistic," said Beau. "That's the word, optimistic."

"But when I was at your house, he said it was your mother who was dragging her feet about going to the doctor."

Beau looked up at me like he just remembered I was there.

"That's Pa for you," said Beau. "He tells you one thing when what he means is just the opposite. *He* was the one who decided we didn't have the money for doctors. Not Ma. He kept saying she'd get better on her own."

"I liked him when I was at your house, Beau. He had neat eyebrows."

Beau smiled. "I like him, too, Lou. I like him a lot."

"So when did you start stealing stuff?" I asked.

"Last year, just after I turned thirteen," Beau said, staring past me into the emptiness of the barn. "We'd moved into a trailer someplace in northern Vermont. Pa kept talking about finding work at this ski resort. He'd keep the ski tow running and I'd do the janitor work for the lodge. Pa told everyone I was sixteen. He's always lying about my age. Since I'm tall, I can get away with it.

"See, it was December and it was freezing outside and our trailer had more holes than a sponge. Ma was trying to make do with two thin sweaters and a blanket. One day a lady comes into the ski lodge wearing this heavy blue jacket with a hood and fur inside. Looking at her fancy clothes you'd guess she probably had two or three more back home. So," said Beau, his eyes meeting mine, "I just snitched her jacket, lifted it right off the rack. Told Ma it was from last year's lost-and-found. Told her the manager at the lodge said I could have it."

"Wow!" I said. "You took it? Just like that?"

I found myself thinking of the sweater Mother had knit me once. It took her almost a whole year to finish it. Somebody stole it out of the front seat of the Jeep by the poultry pavilion at the Bangor State Fair.

"Yes," said Beau, "I took it. I figured Ma needed it more than the other lady did."

"And didn't your father ever find out?"

"Oh, I think he knew. I think he knew the whole time. Especially when the lady made a huge fuss with the manager."

"But didn't he make you take it back?"

"Why should he?" Beau said evenly. "You see, there was no choice. We were out of cash. And Ma was cold."

"Oh, Beau, that's terrible!" I said. "Having to steal stuff, being afraid of getting caught all the time. I don't understand. I couldn't bear it."

"It's hard to understand," said Beau. "I don't even understand it myself sometimes."

He rested his forehead on his knees for a moment.

"That was just the first time," he continued, his gaze fixed on his feet. Then he told me about the other times. The shoes from Sears, Roebuck for his father, the blue jeans, and the spare tire for the truck. The last time he had been working as stock boy at some auto repair shop outside of Boston.

"Can't you make yourself stop? Can't you decide to quit, cold turkey?"

"I mean to stop," said Beau. "I really do. I tell myself every time. This is it. This is the last time for sure. But then something comes up. And Pa don't have the money and don't show any signs of getting it."

Beau brushed the hair off his forehead. There were little pieces of grass sticking out over his ear. His eyes were sad.

"Them magazines from Muldoon's. Ma was getting so down, coughing and coughing like to die. Pa wouldn't do nothing about it, saying for sure she'd be getting better. So stupid me, I decide maybe if I find her something to cheer her up, maybe she will get better. She always likes thumbing through them magazines, staring at the fancy houses and pretty clothes. So that's why you saw me at Muldoon's."

I was glad Beau was telling me all this, but in some ways I didn't want to hear it.

"And that's why you took the cough medicine from the A&P," I said softly.

Beau nodded. "You know, Lou, if I can just nail down a regular paying job somewhere, I think we could make it. I hate this stealing. It's all wrong. And if I get caught . . ."

Our eyes met again.

"Your father said he'd talk to Mr. Farrell about helping out with the mowing," said Beau. "I want to try it. I might be able to start next week."

"Oh, Beau! That's great."

"Yeah," said Beau. "I like your old man. He's neat."

Across the road we could hear the steady crunch of tires on the driveway and people shouting goodbye. The circus was almost over.

Beau cradled his chin in his hands and looked at me. "I been talking your ear off, Lou. I don't know what got into me. I ain't usually like this."

"Oh, I don't mind, I really don't," I said. "It helps to have somebody to talk to."

The rafters creaked, and we listened to the muffled cackle of the chickens in a faraway corner of the barn.

"You were a real hit today, Beau," I said. "You were the best part of the whole circus."

"I wasn't too bad, was I?" said Beau.

"You were great. Even Stephanie thought so."

"Your father gave me most of the ideas."

"Heck, I know that. We've heard all of them before," I said. "Father's been doing the same corny jokes for years."

I got to my feet.

"I guess I'll go back to the house," I said. "You coming?"

We climbed carefully down the hay, anchoring our feet in the cracks between the bales. Beau went first and held out his hand to me as I jumped down the last few inches.

"You know, Lou. I've never told anybody this stuff before. It's nice to have somebody listen."

Beau was still holding my hand. I barely came up to his shirt pocket. "Thanks for tipping me off about Muldoon. I'll pay you back, somehow. I really will."

Suddenly I felt all mixed up. Beau was lonely. He needed a friend, someone he could tell things to, who would try to understand. With no questions asked. Even though I knew I could never steal any-

109

thing, I had to try to understand why he did. And not tell on him. Everything seemed complicated. I wanted to be honest, and somehow I felt like I was becoming part of his dishonesty.

I caught sight of myself in the reflection of the barn window. I realized I hadn't washed off my clown makeup yet and was still wearing the orange wig. I looked ridiculous. I tugged my hand out of Beau's and ran toward the house.

"Beat you to the back door!" I hollered over my shoulder.

That night I was still thinking about our conversation as I lay in the darkness waiting for sleep. Beau's world seemed so different from mine. I'd grown up with friends, pets, piano lessons, Sunday school, picnics, books, and a million other things that he'd never known. I had other kids in my family and a father with a good job and nobody sick. Yet Beau had been all over the country and worked for real money like grown-ups. He had seen things and done things and suffered in a way I couldn't even imagine. Stephanie was right. Beau wasn't like us.

The lights had been out for fifteen minutes, but Stephanie was still tossing and turning. It was a warm night. The air was hot and sticky.

"Rats," Stephanie said out loud.

"Rats?" I waited for her to continue.

"Yeah, rats. I don't think anyone will ever remember the hula dance and the trapeze act from the circus, do you, Lou?"

"They'll remember it, Stephanie. I liked the way you hung from one knee at the very end."

"Oh, sure."

"No, I did. It was great."

"The problem is, Beau was greater," said Stephanie.

"He was pretty good." My sister had called him "Beau" for the first time. Not "Beauregard," but "Beau."

"Jennie was cute, wasn't she?"

"Yeah, she was cute."

I waited. I could tell Stephanie had something on her mind.

"Beau wouldn't have been nearly as good if Mother and Father hadn't helped him with his lines."

"You're probably right," I said.

"I mean, how the heck would a kid like Beau know about ancient Greeks and all that?"

"Right," I said. "He told me afterward that Father had helped him."

A car drove by outside, its headlights throwing a moving shadow of a window across the wall.

"Lou, do you believe all those stories about Beau?"

"Stories?"

"You know, about setting fires and stuff, those stories that were going around at school? Do you believe he really did any of that?"

111

"Do you?" I said.

Stephanie sighed. "When you get right down to it, I guess not."

"That's good," I said.

"I wonder why he tried to shoplift at the A&P?"

"Who knows," I said. "He must have had his reasons."

I didn't want to tell Stephanie about the things Beau had said to me in the barn. For one thing, it seemed like a private conversation. And for another thing, I didn't want her to think any worse of him. But most of all I was hoping that if I didn't tell anybody, the bad parts wouldn't seem so true.

"You know what?" said Stephanie. "I feel stupid that I locked up all our junk. And I'm sort of sorry he's going tomorrow, aren't you?"

"Yes," I said, "in a way." I ran my fingers over the embroidered edge of my pillowcase.

Stephanie yawned. "By the way, you did great on the fortune teller stuff."

"Thanks," I said. "I never repeated the same thing twice."

"That's good," she said. "You did just like I told you."

She turned over. In a few minutes I could hear the steady breathing that told me she was asleep. But I lay awake a long time afterward looking at the stars and thinking of the many things Beau had told me.

CHAPTER NINE

irst thing next morning, Beau wadded up his clothes and stuffed them into a paper bag to take home. Father talked to him about odd jobs he'd had before, so he'd know what to tell Mr. Farrell when asking about work. Mother packed up a huge food basket plus a stack of old *Good Housekeeping* magazines for Beau's mother. Jennie stuck to Beau like a piece of bubble gum.

"Will you come over and see us, Beau? Will you come over again real soon?"

"Oh, sure. I'll be around, Jen." He grinned as he patted her on the head.

"I'm going to learn lots of new tricks on my tricycle. Figure eights and zigzags and lots more!"

"I wouldn't want to miss any new tricks," Beau laughed. "You wait, I'll be over to see you one of these days."

The rest of us crowded around the Jeep as Father and Beau climbed in.

"You keep in touch," said Mother. "The girls will

hear lots of compliments on your performance in the circus. They'll want to pass them along."

"Thanks," said Beau.

"I hope your mother feels better," said Stephanie. Nobody wanted to say good-bye. Not even Stephanie.

"Well, I better get going," said Beau at last. "Thanks for everything, Mrs. Berry. I really appreciated it. So long, everybody."

Beau leaned out the Jeep window, resting one arm on the sill. Our eyes met and he smiled. I wanted to say something special, but I didn't know what. Something special, but not too special. I stood a few feet away from the Jeep and fumbled through my mind for the right words. The Jeep had started to roll down the driveway.

"I'm glad we talked, Beau!" I shouted in desperation.

But my voice was lost in the motor's chugging. Father was already halfway to the road. I didn't know whether Beau heard me or not.

I kicked a stone idly up the gravel driveway. Stephanie and Jennie waved from the back step. The Jeep passed the Farrells' and disappeared out of sight around the bend. I strained my ears to catch the last noise of the motor.

We didn't see much of Beau after that. The same day he left, Father arranged for him to work at the Farrells' dairy farm for the rest of the summer. Mr.

Farrell needed an extra hand with the mowing and milking now that his own two boys were up at the lumber mill. Soon we saw Beau weaving back and forth across the field on the tractor, the baling machine spitting out chunks of hay like giant shoe boxes. Other times he'd be rounding up the cows for milking, or pitching bales onto the hay wagon. After a few days Mr. Farrell told Father that Beau worked steady as a clock compared to his own boys.

Sometimes we walked over to the fence. Beau would bring Jennie something he'd been saving for her— a faded ribbon from one of the Farrells' prize-winning cows, or the cellophane from an old cigarette wrapper he'd picked up at the side of the road. We'd stand around talking about the circus or Crowberry's new tricks. Beau seemed glad to see us.

"Did you catch Mr. Keene's radio mystery last night, Beau?" Stephanie would ask.

"Nope. 'Fraid I missed it," Beau would reply, chewing thoughtfully on a stalk of timothy grass and listening while Stephanie rambled on about the lady who found the poisonous snake in her bed or the man who went for a walk along a cliff on a stormy night and never came back.

"How's your mother doing?" I'd ask.

"She's coming along just fine," he'd say.

Then Jennie would start in telling him about dumb stuff you knew he couldn't possibly care about. Like all the names of the kids in her Sunday school class

115

or how come she decided to wear her white shirt instead of her red one. Beau would smile and nod all the way through when she retold her bedtime story of the night before.

"You mean that little pig rolled down a steep hill in a barrel?" he'd ask, lifting his eyebrows in stunned disbelief.

"Hey, why don't you wear that shirt with the balloons on it, Jen," he'd suggest. "I sure do like them balloons."

We knew he was glad to see us, even if he didn't say it in so many words. He was quiet. That was just his style.

Stephanie and I were leaving for Girl Scout camp soon, but somehow we didn't want to go as much as we had in other years. At least I didn't. I knew I'd miss Beau.

The day before camp, something happened that changed everything. When I first heard Stephanie talking over the phone to Jody, I figured she was calling us back to thank us for inviting her to the circus. So it came as a surprise when Stephanie cupped the receiver in her hand and called, "Lou, did anyone find a twenty-dollar bill in the garage? After the circus on Saturday?"

I caught my breath. Twenty dollars. In the garage. With Beau.

"Jody thinks it may have dropped out of her purse during the sideshow. When she was getting her money for Beau's act. She's not sure." Stephanie continued, "It was birthday money she'd been saving. From her uncle Pat. You know, Mr. Muldoon."

Not again, I thought. Has Beau taken something from the Muldoons? I quickly pushed the thought from my mind.

Stephanie told Jody we'd take a look and call her right back. Then we searched every inch of the garage—under the empty chicken coops along one wall, in the toolbox, behind the garbage cans, beneath the scraps of tar paper on the floor, in the pile in the corner where we'd dropped our sideshow costumes and hadn't bothered to pick them up. There was no sign of a twenty-dollar bill.

"I'll bet he took it," Stephanie said, half to herself and half to me. Her forehead wrinkled into a frown.

"Not Beau. I know he wouldn't take the money, Stephanie," I said, spitting out the words without even thinking of them.

"But it would be so tempting for him to pick it up," she said. "To slide it into his pocket when nobody was watching."

"Oh, no, Stephanie, I doubt it. Maybe Jody lost her money in the car. Or the wind could have blown it out into the grass. The garage was wide open. And somebody at the circus, one of the town kids, probably picked it up."

My mind was cranking out solutions as fast as it could. It couldn't be Beau. Not after the way we'd talked in the barn. It just couldn't be Beau.

"How can you be so sure he didn't do it?" asked Stephanie.

"Well, for one thing, he didn't act guilty or suspicious. Right? During the animal act, he acted perfectly normal. And for another thing, all week he seemed like he was really trying to fit in. Helping Mother and all that. Somebody who is trying to fit in doesn't go around stealing things."

I was trying to sound convincing. But what I was saying and what I was thinking didn't match up. It would take only a split second to hide a twenty dollar bill in your pocket. And Beau needed money. What if he had seen it fall onto the dirt floor of the garage? Why wouldn't he have scooped it up after the other kids had filed out? Twenty dollars could buy an awful lot—medicine, food, gas for the truck, warm blankets for cold winter nights.

"I suppose the A&P thing could have been an isolated incident," said Stephanie slowly.

"Isolated incident?" I said. "What do you mean?"

"You know, a one-time thing."

Right, I thought. A one-time thing. If Stephanie knew what I knew, she wouldn't believe Beau was innocent at all.

"I suppose we could ask Beau if he saw it," I said, letting my fears creep into my voice for the first time.

"Listen, you can't ask him straight out like that. He'd think we were accusing him of something. You

118

don't go around making your friends uncomfortable, do you?"

"No, I guess not," I said.

I could tell Stephanie was just as confused as I was. She didn't want to think Beau was a thief either.

"It's been over a week since the circus. She could have lost her money a lot of other places," I said suddenly, hoping to think of a way out for Beau.

"That's what I said to her," said Stephanie gloomily. "But she says that was the only time she's had that purse out. It's her special purse, just for parties."

"Darn," I said. "Did Jody mention Beau on the telephone?" I asked. "Did she hint that he might have taken it, I mean?"

"Yes, she did. She said she was pretty sure where she'd look for the money, and had we noticed that 'blarney' and 'Carney' rhymed." Stephanie sighed.

"Drat. I know what that means. Beau's name will be as good as mud."

I could see Jody and her uncle spreading the word far and wide that Beauregard Carney was crooked as a corkscrew. Mr. Muldoon would be thrilled. He'd have another bad-kid horror story to tell at the store.

"Well, there's only one thing to do," said Stephanie matter-of-factly. "We'll have to get twenty dollars of our own money and pretend we found it in the garage. That way, if the money turns up, we can keep it and everyone's even. And if it doesn't—"

"Beau is off the hook," I said.

Like I said, Stephanie and I had been saving our Christmas and birthday money for a year, and we had forty dollars between us. Next time we went to Ellbridge, we would leave a folded twenty-dollar bill in an envelope at Muldoon's Drug Store for Jody. It was crazy, but there didn't seem to be any other way of keeping the Ellbridge gossips away from Beau.

"As far as I'm concerned, that finishes it," said Stephanie. "If he took it, he took it, and there's nothing we can do about it." She went back to the house to phone Jody that we'd found the money.

As far as I was concerned, it was a big fat cover-up and we both knew it. I walked across the road to the barn. I wondered why Stephanie didn't brood about things the way I did. It didn't seem to matter to her anymore that Beau was a thief.

If only I could talk to him. Just to find out one way or the other. But we were getting up bright and early tomorrow to drive to camp, and I knew I wouldn't see Beau until I got back. Besides, Stephanie was right. You can't ask people whether they've stolen something. You shouldn't even think bad things about someone if he's really your friend.

On the roof, Crowberry perched motionless. If it hadn't been for Crow, we might never have met the Carneys, I thought. Father would never have dropped by Beau's house. Mrs. Carney might be getting worse instead of better. A lot worse.

"Here, Crowberry! Come here!" I called. Crowberry lifted off and coasted to my shoulder.

"Hey, what do you say?" I whispered softly to the bird. "Let's pretend the twenty dollars never happened." But even as I said the words, I knew I couldn't make myself forget. I could never feel quite the same about Beau, no matter how hard I tried.

Crow's claws dug into my shoulder, and he tugged at the barrette in my hair.

"Ouch! Don't do that!" I cried. "It hurts."

CHAPTER TEN

We were at camp for over a month. I wrote Jennie a postcard twice a week. Mother and Father came to see us once. When we asked Mother about Beau, she said that he was mowing the lawn for us while we were gone and that Crow was spending a lot of time at the Carneys' and the Farrells', following him around while he did his chores.

I often wondered if he'd spent the twenty dollars, but then I'd tell myself for the hundredth time that we didn't know for sure that he'd taken it. Not absolutely one hundred percent for certain.

That summer Stephanie moved in with a whole new bunch of girls since she was going into seventh grade in the fall. They wore lipstick and fixed their hair in different hairstyles every day. They giggled a lot and stayed up late talking about the boys on the kitchen staff. Then they talked about the boys at the Boy Scout camp across the lake. Then the boys back home. They didn't seem all that interested in earning merit badges. I heard her mention Beau's name once or twice.

Camp Wahaco was overstocked on gimp that summer. I made a gimp bracelet, a gimp watchband, a key chain, a headband, a belt, and a lanyard. There was a ton of gimp left over, so I saved extra for Jennie to make a leash for Micky. Besides that, I got my swimming and outdoor-cooking badges. But to tell the truth I was counting the days till camp was over. I wanted to come home to Crowberry, Jennie, and Beau.

When we finally returned in the middle of August, Crow was waiting for us. He dive-bombed the car as we rolled up the driveway, and drummed on every window in the house waiting for us to come out and play with him. He had learned a new trick while we were gone—holding down a newspaper with one foot and jerking strips off the side with his beak. He could shred a sheet of comics in five minutes flat. We wondered whether he would leave us in the fall. Other crows were joining up in groups of twos or threes, getting ready to fly south.

Once he tried to make friends with the sea gulls that gathered to look for worms in the field across the road. Worms weren't that easy to find. It was a dry summer. But the gulls ignored him like an uninvited guest at a party. Crow looked silly flapping his wings to keep up as they hung motionless like sleek white gliders in the sky. After two or three days he gave up and flew back to his lonely post in the pine tree.

After camp Jennie and Beau were even better friends than ever. At first Jennie had picked bouquets of dandelions every few days and trotted them over to Mrs. Carney. But after a while she went over to the Carneys' any old time she felt like it. Mother was worried she'd make a pest of herself, but Beau said his mother didn't get out all that much and loved the company.

The first time we saw Beau after our return was the day he showed up at our house to pick up his pay for mowing the lawn. We all stood around awkwardly in the kitchen. It's hard when you haven't seen somebody for a long time. Beau's hair was trimmed neatly around his ears, and he looked like he'd grown an inch taller. He and Mother figured out his hours, and he added them up on a little notebook he had in his pocket. It was pretty businesslike to me. Beau seemed older, now that I saw him working for real money.

"Did you get my postcard, Beau?" asked Stephanie in an odd voice. I didn't know she'd sent him one.

"Oh, yeah. The postcard. Yeah. I got it all right. Thanks. Thanks a lot, Stephanie." He filed the money carefully away in his wallet.

"When does school start for the Lawrence children?" asked Mother.

"Day after Labor Day," said Beau.

Beau was as tongue-tied as ever. So Mother had another go at him. "Are you looking forward to school?"

"I guess so," said Beau. "I don't know the kids too well yet."

"Bring in baseball cards," said Jennie. "That's what I'm going to do. Then you'll get to know a whole bunch."

Jennie was starting kindergarten in September and was worried about making friends herself. Beau smiled. "Don't worry, Jen. Those school kids are going to love you. Anybody that knows the tricks you do, why, you'll wow 'em!"

Jennie looked pleased.

Mother glanced at her watch. "Good gracious! We'll be late again. Stephanie, get your music and meet me in the car." It was Stephanie's piano lesson. "Lou, you're in charge. We should be back in an hour. Pick some lettuce while I'm gone, will you, dear?"

Stephanie gathered up her music and followed Mother out the door. As she passed Beau, she paused, peering at him out of the corner of her eyes, like a lady in a lipstick ad. "I was wondering if you'd like to see Marty's pictures from the circus?"

"Pictures?"

"Yes, Marty is going to give some to me. She said you were in quite a few. I thought you might like to come over sometime and see them."

Beau cleared his throat. "Oh, that's nice. Great."

Stephanie waited for him to say something else.

"I haven't been in too many pictures before," said Beau.

Mother tooted the horn. Stephanie was still hanging on.

"Well," said Beau. "Guess I'd better get on home."

He nodded at Jennie and me and slipped out the door. Stephanie followed him out without a word. We heard the car doors slam, and gradually the noise of the motor faded. The house seemed empty.

"Hey, wait!" said Jennie, seized with a sudden inspiration. "I didn't show Beau my new tricks." Quick as a flash she raced outside calling after him.

I pulled the garden basket from under the sink and headed for the lettuce patch in the backyard. Beau was at the mailbox, but Jennie was begging and pleading. Out of the corner of my eye I could see him coming back up the driveway, following Jennie as she zigzagged toward the swings like a butterfly, darting ahead, then returning to say something to Beau, then skipping ahead, then scurrying back again.

I slid my fingers in among the lettuce plants. The leaves were dry and gritty and the soil packed hard as rock. We needed rain. I broke the tops off the taller plants, which were spiraling into seed, and pinched off the greener leaves and put them into the basket. Jennie hung upside down from the trapeze, and Beau whistled and cheered. Now and then his words floated to me over the breeze.

The first thing I'd done when I got home from camp was to check the "Police Blotter" column in the back issues of the *Ellbridge American* to make sure there was nothing about a fourteen-year-old boy. I had to be certain that Beau was finished with shoplifting. I looked through six issues, but I didn't find a thing.

Look for good, not evil, in people. That's what Mother's note to Stephanie had said. Know what to overlook. I was trying hard, but I couldn't make myself forget Jody's twenty-dollar bill.

"How was camp?"

I looked up. Beau was standing a few feet away, grinning at me. His arms rested on the garden gate, brown as caramel. In the distance, Jennie was hollering at Beau to watch her.

"Camp was okay," I said. I told him about the egg-salad soup we had for supper at the mess hall. Beau smiled. I told him that Stephanie and I got to carry the flags at the awards ceremony.

"Oh, yeah? And did you earn any badges?"

"I did. But Stephanie didn't."

"How come?"

"I think she went boy crazy on us this summer instead," I said.

Beau chuckled. "And how about you, Lou?"

"Are you kidding? Not me," I said. I began pulling out the weeds around the lettuce plants. "I hate boys."

Beau shifted the gate back and forth with his foot. He had dimples in his cheeks when he smiled.

"That's too bad," he said.

I pulled rocks out of the dirt and tossed them to one side. Jennie was on her hands and knees, edging along the ladder that ran along the top of the swings.

"Good, Jen. Pretty tricky," called Beau. He held his hands over his head and clapped again. Somebody had patched his sleeves in the elbows. It was the same old blue-gray shirt he'd worn the first time I saw him, in Muldoon's stealing magazines. Suddenly I knew I couldn't wait any longer.

"Beau," I said, sitting up straight. "There's something I have to ask you."

"Sure. Go ahead. Shoot." His eyes crinkled at the corners.

"It's about the circus, the sideshow. You know, last June."

Beau was watching me with interest.

"Jody lost some money. A twenty-dollar bill, actually. She's sure she dropped it out of her purse, during the sideshow. In the garage."

Beau's body stiffened.

"The thing is, I was wondering if . . . what I wanted to know was . . . did you, I mean, were you . . . ?"

Beau dropped his eyes to the ground. Then he straightened up and looked away toward the mountains and the river.

"So you think I took it," he said to no one in particular.

"It's not that, Beau. I was just wondering if you'd seen it."

"No, I didn't see it, Lou," he said softly. "I would have given it back to you if I'd seen it."

Everything in his manner had changed. Jennie was turning cartwheels on the grass and shouting to Beau, but he wasn't paying attention. It was like a shade had been drawn down between us.

"Hey, Beau! Look! This is my very, very best one! One foot," yelled Jennie. She was dangling from the rings like a monkey.

"Not bad, Jen!" he called. "One more trick and I gotta go." He started back toward the swing.

"Wait a minute!" I jumped up and ran after him. "I never said you took the money. I just wanted to know . . ."

Beau was pulled in tighter than a clam in a shell.

"I'm sorry, Beau," I said, trailing after him. "I didn't mean to say anything bad."

"No big deal," he said, shrugging his shoulders. "Don't worry about it, okay?"

"I just thought you might have seen it."

"Sure, I know," said Beau bitterly. "I'm the likely suspect, right? The only criminal you know. Listen.

Ma's waiting. I have to be off now."

He jammed his hands into his pockets and strode toward the mailbox. When he reached the road he turned back.

"Louise!"

I felt a pang somewhere near my heart.

"Tell your father the mower needs gas."

"Okay," I shouted. I watched until Beau's tiny figure disappeared around the bend.

I went upstairs and sprawled on my bed. I'd been waiting to see Beau all summer and now I'd ruined everything. The more I thought about our conversation, the more I realized I had been wrong not to trust him. Of course he didn't take the money. Why hadn't I listened to Stephanie? You don't accuse people of things without any evidence. Why couldn't I keep my big mouth shut? Tears trickled down my cheeks into my ears.

I traced the pattern on the wallpaper with my finger, garlands of tiny blue flowers looped and tangled with no beginning and no end. Why was I so crazy about Beau? Something as fragile as a house of cards existed between us. I'd felt it the very first time, in Muldoon's.

Beau had been through a lot. He was tough. But between us was something so delicate it could shatter in an instant if you weren't careful. Like tiny pieces of colored glass in a kaleidoscope, which tumble into disarray if you jiggle your hand. Or the rainbow-colored soap bubble, which vanishes if you blow too hard. I'd glimpsed this mysterious thing and I knew it was something fine, and rare, and wonderful. Now it was gone.

My eyes were still red when Mother and Stephanie came back from the lesson. I told them I'd had a sneezing fit from hay fever. They shouldn't worry. I'd be all right in a while.

CHAPTER ELEVEN

*S*onny Farrell wasn't all that much to look at—stocky and black haired, with pants slung so low on his hips that you wished he'd pull in his belt one notch tighter. He had a funny pointy head, and when he laughed you could see two rows of greenish-yellow teeth, tiny as dried peas. I guess he wasn't more than nineteen or twenty.

Sonny had a reputation to keep up. In town he was about as popular as a skunk at a lawn party. Some people claimed Sonny had a real mean streak, but others said he just liked a good joke. Along with his younger brother, Clarence, he kept things stirred up livelier than the people in Ellbridge were used to.

It was Sonny who plastered the JESUS SAVES signs all over the front of the Ellbridge National Bank. And Sonny who put goldfish in the toilets in the ladies' room at the Ellbridge High School Senior Prom. While the girls in their prom dresses were shrieking at their boyfriends, Sonny and Clarence were out in the parking lot turning everybody's license plates upside down.

Father said Sonny and Clarence didn't have an ounce of common sense. That's why Mr. Farrell had sent them up to the lumber mill after they graduated, to see if hard work would straighten them out. The way Mother explained it, Mrs. Farrell had died a long time ago, so Sonny and Clarence had never had much supervision growing up. They'd pretty much run wild ever since we'd known them. If we woke up and found our front lawn full of cows walking around loose, we could be pretty sure who did it.

About two weeks after we returned from camp, I got a telephone call from Mr. Farrell.

"You girls still got that pet crow over there?"

"Yes, we do."

"Sits on fence posts, does he? Comes right up to your shoulder, does he? Flies over here with Beau Carney?" Half the stuff Mr. Farrell said was a question.

As Mother had told us at camp, Crow had been following Beau around ever since we left. I missed Beau. He hadn't been over since our talk in the lettuce patch.

"It's Sonny and Clarence I got to tell you about. They got a vacation from the lumber mill for a few days. Knowing them like I do, I'm sure they'll be wanting to do some shooting, don't you know?"

"Gee, Mr. Farrell, the deer season doesn't begin until November."

"Deer? Oh, the boys go out for the fun of it. Why, they'll take a shot at anything that moves. Heck, squirrel is legal September first, ain't it? Rabbit? Duck? They don't care. It's for the fun of it."

I gulped, wondering how we could keep Crowberry at home. I remembered Drummer's bandaged leg at Dr. Butler's office.

"Oh, I'll tell 'em about your crow. But it may not do much good. Just thought I'd better warn you." Mr. Farrell hung up.

You had to feel sorry for old Mr. Farrell. Sonny and Clarence really gave him problems. The balloons on Memorial Day were the last straw. The boys had filled balloons with water up on the roof of the A&P and lobbed them down on their friends marching by in the parade. One of the balloons caught the fire chief, Sparky Grindle, in the neck. Mr. Farrell was on the phone the next day lining up out-of-town jobs at the lumber mill for his sons.

Stephanie frowned as I repeated Mr. Farrell's warning. "Now how are we supposed to keep Crow away from the Farrells'?"

"Maybe Father can explain to the boys," I said. "Maybe he'll take us over after supper tonight."

Usually we had "Cow Night" at the Farrells' dairy barn at least once a month anyway. We stopped by the dairy, and while Father and Mr. Farrell talked about cows and chickens, Stephanie, Jennie, and I wandered around in the barn. Mr. Farrell had about fifty cows in stalls along both sides of a central aisle. It was funny and fascinating to watch them arch their backs, lift their tails, and deliver huge brown plops of manure with a splat only a few feet away from where we were standing.

When that got boring you could sneak down to the far end of the barn and peer around the corner, where an enormous bull was tied up. And in the spring there were usually a dozen spindly-legged calves to pet. When it was chilly, we burrowed down inside the roomful of sawdust Mr. Farrell kept to dust the floors, up to our necks like sunbathers in the sand.

As we pulled into the Farrells', Drummer bounded out to meet us, his tail wagging his whole body. Sonny's hot rod was parked at a jaunty angle, blocking the driveway. The words TO HELL OR BUST were painted in red-and-gold letters on the side. Silver flames curled around the wheels, and a pair of oversized dice dangled from the front mirror. There was no sign of Sonny and Clarence.

"Well, Doc, how ya' doing?"

Lloyd Farrell wiped his hands on his handkerchief and clapped Father around the shoulders. His gray hair was trimmed as neat as the bushes around his house.

"Can you come in and see my new milking machine? I'm just oiling her up."

Father disappeared into the barn. Stephanie stayed behind to help Jennie tie her shoe. We were about to follow when all of a sudden we heard a funny tapping sound coming from behind the milk house. Sonny Farrell was hobbling toward us on crutches.

"Sonny!" exclaimed Stephanie. "What happened to you?"

"Nothin' much," said Sonny. He was hanging real low on the crutches, and his leg was wound in white bandages clear up to his thigh as tight as a mummy. He smiled at us, screwing up his little black eyes and grinning so you could see every beany tooth in his head. His black hair curled down over his forehead like a woolly cap.

"Got my leg run over just last week," he muttered, shaking his head. "Broke in three different places."

"Whew!" winced Stephanie. "I'll bet it hurt something awful."

"I thought I was a goner for a while there," said Sonny. "Felt pretty peaked. But I'm better now. Just got to take it easy."

I stared at Sonny's leg, trying to figure out how somebody could get one leg run over and not the other.

"So how's everything at the Berrys'?" said Sonny. "Bet it's been pretty boring around here without Clarence and me to keep things hopping." He limped a few steps, dragging his leg behind him. We could see his toes poking out the end of the bandage.

I was just about to tell him about Crow when Clarence appeared in the doorway, lugging a couple of milk cans. While Sonny was dark, Clarence was pale as dishwater. He had pink, rabbity eyes.

"Hey, bufflehead. You and work have a falling out or something?" Clarence didn't bother to say hello to us. Sonny sagged lower on his crutches.

"Get in here and help me with these chores, Sonny!" There was an edge to Clarence's words that made me uncomfortable.

"Work?" said Sonny. "You expect me to work in my condition? I'm supposed to be resting up. The doctor says so."

"You could make a good living, bottoming chairs," snorted Clarence.

"Will you get off my back, Clarence! My leg's broke in three places, for cryin' out loud! I got to use these crutches for two more months!"

Sonny was building up a head of steam. Jennie looked worried, so I reached over and squeezed her hand.

"Trying to weasel out again, are ya'?" said Clarence. "We'll see about that, you good-for-nothing loafer!"

He picked up a stone off the driveway and shot it at Sonny's bad leg. His brother howled in pain, dropped his crutches, and fell moaning on the driveway. It was horrible. Jennie hid her eyes in my sweater.

"Quick! Get Father!" shouted Stephanie. "Sonny and Clarence are going to kill each other!"

We dashed for the barn and hollered for Father and Mr. Farrell. Outside, Clarence had picked up Sonny's crutch and was trying to bash him over the head with it.

"He's hitting Sonny's sore leg!" screamed Jennie, too fascinated to turn away. The boys were rolling over and over on the driveway belting each other. They were almost invisible in the cloud of dust.

"You stupid clodhopper!" gasped Sonny. "You asked for it!" He had managed to get on top of Clarence and had pinned his arms to his sides. He seemed to have forgotten all about his leg.

Mr. Farrell hurried out to the barnyard and stared in wonder at his battling sons.

"What in God's name are you two doing?" he yelled. He rushed over and pried them apart. "Get that foolish bed sheet off your leg, Sonny, and get in here and give me a hand with these cows!"

Bed sheet?

"Oh, Mr. Farrell," said Jennie. "That's not a bed sheet. That's a bandage. His leg is broken in three places! It got run over!"

Mr. Farrell stepped back and rubbed his hand on the back of his neck. Sonny and Clarence pulled themselves up laughing. Sonny's leg was strong as a tree trunk. He wasn't any lamer than I was. It looked like we'd been had. Stephanie and I glanced at each other. We didn't know whether to laugh or not. Jennie still hadn't figured it out.

"Hey, how'd you like our little show? Did we have you girls snookered?"

Sonny chuckled. Then he dusted off his pant leg. His brother was grinning too as he shook the dirt out of his shirt.

"See, honey?" said Clarence, reaching over and tugging the torn sheeting off Sonny's leg for Jennie to see. "Ain't nothing wrong with that leg. It's the face that's the problem. 'Fraid this fella was in the back row when they passed out the faces!"

He hooted with laughter as Sonny slammed his fist into his shoulder. Jennie didn't crack a smile. She didn't like to be fooled.

"Hey, Clarence, want to try it out on Main Street? Come on!" Sonny finished peeling the sheet off his leg.

"How you boys expect to get ahead in this world is beyond me," said Mr. Farrell, wagging his finger at his sons.

But the boys paid no attention to Mr. Farrell. They were already loading the crutches and bandages into the hot rod. We watched as Sonny's car lurched out of the driveway and sped down the road toward Ellbridge.

"You sure have your hands full with that pair, Lloyd," said Father.

"They're asking for it, Doc. I know they don't mean no harm. But I swear, the next prank they pull I'm kicking them right out of the house. I'm too old for their shenanigans."

Mr. Farrell wiped his handkerchief over his forehead and walked slowly back to the cows. He looked completely tuckered out.

"Why were Sonny and Clarence acting so silly? They scared me," said Jennie when we were on our way home.

"That's the way they are. Sometimes you just have to take people the way they are," I said, thinking suddenly of Beau.

"Let's have some popcorn when we get home," said Stephanie.

It was almost dark. The pine trees were etched like black lace against the fading sunset. As soon as the Jeep stopped in the driveway, Jennie jumped out and raced into the house.

"Oh, Mother, Sonny played a terrible trick!"

Mother listened quietly to Jennie. Stephanie got out the popcorn and began heating the oil in the pan. I walked out to the back porch and studied the branches of the pine tree, looking for Crow. I felt uneasy, thinking about Sonny and Clarence living right next door. I knew I wouldn't relax until the boys were back at the lumber mill.

It took a while for my eyes to get used to the dark. The pine branches whispered restlessly in the cool

night air. Finally, I spotted Crow's dark figure sil-
houetted in the fading light. He was perched far out
on a long bough, halfway up the tree, like a popgun
target at a carnival booth waiting to be shot.

CHAPTER TWELVE

I still felt uneasy the next morning. Mother was still reassuring Jennie about Sonny and Clarence's trick. Probably they had already returned to the lumber mill, she said. All the same, I noticed that Sonny's hot rod was parked in the driveway when we went by on our way into town the next day.

Even after a long summer, the town kids had not forgotten Beau. Marty and Jody kept bugging Stephanie about him. Did he ever come over to our house? Had he taught Crowberry any new tricks? Did he buy any new clothes with the money from Mr. Farrell? Stephanie clammed up. She told the girls she didn't give two hoots about Beauregard Carney.

But of course I knew she did. She stared out the Jeep window as hard as the rest of us when we drove by Beau's house. And she asked Father if he thought there was a chance Mrs. Carney might go back to the hospital so that Beau would have to come to our house again. He said Mrs. Carney was doing fine.

A couple of days after Sonny played his trick, Mother announced that she had saved a stack of old *Saturday Evening Post*s from Father's office for Mrs. Carney. Stephanie begged to take them over. I knew she hoped to catch a glimpse of Beau. School was due to start up again in a week, and I guess she figured she wouldn't get to talk to him after that. I'd never seen anyone brush her hair quite so long just to deliver a few dog-eared magazines. When she got to the Carneys', Beau wasn't even there. She had to come back home without seeing him.

"Well?" I said.

"Well, what?"

"Was he over there?"

"Oh, Beau? No, he wasn't. I gave the magazines to his father."

"Too bad," I said.

"Oh, it's all right," said Stephanie. "I'll ask him later."

"Ask him what?" I said.

Stephanie fiddled with her wristwatch.

"Ask him to the party at church next weekend," she said.

"You're going to ask Beauregard Carney to the Youth Fellowship party at church?" I didn't know whether I liked the idea or not. Two months ago Stephanie was calling Beau a juvenile delinquent, and here she was asking him to a church party. Besides, I was afraid he was still mad at me.

"Well, Mr. Munson said we were to try to bring new members to the youth group starting this fall. So why not?"

"I don't know," I said, still trying to puzzle it out. "They'll tease you like crazy."

Ever since the circus, Marty and Jody had been sneaking up behind our backs, whispering silly jingles like "Lou to wed a talking head" and "It's go, go, go, for Steph and Beau!"

"Who cares if they tease me? They're probably just jealous. Besides, I wasn't going to tell them that *I* was asking Beau. I was going to tell them that *we* were asking Beau."

"That we were asking him?" I said.

"Sure, that way we can sort of share the blame," said Stephanie.

"What if he says no?" I asked. "After all, he may not want to go. He probably never set foot inside a church before in his life."

"Oh, he couldn't say no. Not after all we've done for him. You'll see. He's got to say yes. I know he will."

I could still picture the hurt in Beau's eyes over the garden gate.

"So when are you going to ask him? The party is only five days away."

"Tonight," said Stephanie. "We'll walk over and ask him tonight. His father said he'd be home at suppertime." She went into the house, and soon I could hear her playing "Beautiful Dreamer" on the piano.

After dinner Stephanie pushed back her chair and announced that she and I were going over to the Carneys'.

Mother looked up from her coffee. "What's going on at the Carneys'?" Outside, dusk was fast approaching.

Stephanie began clearing the table in a burst of nervous activity, the plates and glasses clattering together.

"Well, I've been thinking a lot about what the minister said about trying to get more kids to go to the youth group at church, and Lou has too, I know, and we were away so much of the summer. We didn't make a thing for the bake sale they had, or go on the hike."

Stephanie was circling round and round the point. She had never asked a boy out before.

"Well, you see how it is. To make a long story short, Lou and I thought we'd ask Beau to the Youth Fellowship party this Saturday."

"What a good idea," Mother exclaimed. "We haven't seen Beau in a long time, and I'd be happy to drive."

"Oh, can I go with the big girls, Mommy?" begged Jennie. "Please, let me go too! I haven't seen Beau in ages!"

But Mother said it was getting late and it was time

for Jennie's bath. Stephanie and I had better get going before it got too dark, and hurry home so we could do the dishes.

We grabbed our jackets and slipped out the door, Jennie's crying growing fainter as we hurried down the driveway, past the mailboxes and the warning sign for Crowberry. It was windier than you'd expect for a late summer night. I had a funny feeling in my stomach. I didn't know how Beau would react when he saw me.

We were a hundred yards from the Farrells' when Stephanie pulled up short.

"Am I seeing things?" she said. "What's that on the Farrells' roof?"

I took a few steps forward, staring at a large wooden object perched precariously on the roof of Mr. Farrell's front porch.

"Whatever it is, it's as big as a refrigerator crate. Bigger even."

We peered at the box. Mr. Farrell's place was always immaculate. He mowed his lawn every three days, and his bushes were always clipped. He probably used a tape measure when he planted his flowers.

Stephanie laughed. "You know what that is, Lou?"

"No," I said. "What is it?"

"It's the Farrells' outhouse!"

"You're kidding!" I giggled. It was the outhouse, all right. When we walked closer, we could see it

146

was their old two-holer, left over from the days when none of the houses on our road had plumbing. It was gray and weatherbeaten, and swayed back and forth ever so slightly in the wind.

"How in the world did it get up on the roof?"

"Oh, come on, Lou. Think!" said Stephanie.

It had to be Sonny and Clarence. They must have hauled it up there when Mr. Farrell was in town.

"Those guys are nuts!" I said. "Their father probably had a fit!"

Sonny's hot rod was nowhere in sight.

"I'll bet Mr. Farrell got fed up and sent the boys back to the lumber mill," I said. "Probably he couldn't stand them anymore."

I walked around the porch looking for clues so I could figure out how the boys had done it. Maybe they'd hitched a rope to the tractor and hoisted it up.

"Will you hurry up?" said Stephanie impatiently. "This doesn't call for a full-scale investigation. Come on. It's getting dark!"

We started off for the Carneys' past the old dirt road into the Farrells' dump. There were tire tracks in the dirt.

"Looks like somebody's been at the dump," I said, kicking at the ruts with my toe. I was stalling for time. Thinking about seeing Beau after all this time was making me nervous. Should I say anything about Jody's money? What if he didn't smile when he saw me? What if he gave me a frozen stare and one-word answers?

"Oh, come on, Lou, will you move?" Stephanie took my elbow and hurried me along. "I want to get this over with," she said firmly.

As soon as we were at the end of the Carneys' driveway, Bozo began to bark. Beau held the door open with one hand and gripped the big dog's collar with the other. We hardly looked at each other in the confusion. Bozo yelped frantically, choking against the leash.

"Shut up, Bozo!" Beau shouted. "Pa said you came over this afternoon. Want anything special?"

The big dog was straining at the collar, but this time I wasn't afraid, because I realized he was good-natured once he'd sniffed you over.

"You can let him go," I shouted. "We don't care if he jumps on us."

Bozo leaped away from Beau, slobbering all over me, his tongue like a soggy washcloth on my face, his paws against my shoulders. I nuzzled the shaggy fur around his neck and tried to keep my balance. Finally I got up my nerve to look at Beau.

He was watching me with a funny smile on his face.

"That dog sure is fond of you, Lou." His mouth curled into a grin.

I felt like black storm clouds had rolled away. I wanted to tell him that I was sorry, that I'd made an awful mistake. That it didn't matter about the money. That I knew I'd botched things up but I'd never do it again. I wanted to tell him all these things, but instead I just grinned back like an idiot, the words stuck in my throat.

"Come on in," said Beau, holding the door for us.

The kitchen was stifling. The wood stove was cranked up high. Stephanie's eyes darted around, taking in the patched linoleum, the secondhand furniture, the bare walls. This was the first time she'd been inside Beau's house. Bozo paced the room, swatting our legs with his big tail and poking his nose into our sides.

"Calm down, Bozo. Be still!"

It was the same frail voice I'd heard once before at the Carneys'. I turned around slowly. A tiny, shriveled-up woman slumped forward in the dirty, overstuffed easy chair in the corner. Her face was the color of library paste and her hands trembled, but I knew the minute she gave us a crinkley-eyed smile that it was Beau's mother.

The *Saturday Evening Post*s that Mother had sent over that afternoon were stacked on the floor next to her chair. I couldn't help it, but I found myself looking around for the other magazines, the ones from Muldoon's. There was a blue jacket with a furry hood hanging from a nail on the wall by the door.

"Come inside, girls. It's dark out there." She spoke with a thick southern accent. "You must be Stephanie and Lou. Beau tells us lots about you girls. He's so fond of you all."

Beau mumbled something and started rubbing Bozo's ears like crazy.

Mrs. Carney told us all about how she grew up in a family of seven kids. She told us where they were living now, and how her father worked till the day he died on a farm in North Carolina. She said she quit high school to take care of her brothers and sisters. We heard that she loved to cook and garden and sew and make persimmon jelly, and how it was a shame her health was failing her so soon.

You could tell she hardly ever got to talk to people. She seemed so happy to see us, her eyes skipping from Stephanie to me and then back again. Her face lit up and her hands fluttered in the air. She'd pick up on a new sentence before the last one was finished. Every so often she lost her breath, and finally, after a fit of coughing, she had to stop.

"Want a drink of water, Ma?" said Beau.

"No, no, Beau. Carry me into the bedroom. My medicine is in there."

We waited as another spasm of coughs rolled from her chest.

"I'm really ever so much better, thanks to your father. I'm so glad to meet you girls. And your parents, too. Kind people," she said. "And your sister Jennie is a peach. I call her my flower girl."

"She's awful cute," said Stephanie. "And I'm glad

150

you're feeling better, Mrs. Carney," she continued in her politest Calvert School voice. "We were all real worried about you."

We stepped back as Beau scooped up his mother, blankets and all, and carried her out of the room.

"Be right back," he called over his shoulder.

When they were gone, Stephanie said, "It's pitch-black outside, and we didn't bring a flashlight."

"And you haven't even asked him yet," I said.

"I know. I will. I'm working up to it." She kept patting her hair and looking at her reflection in the window the way people do when they're nervous.

"Well, you'd better hurry up."

"I will," said Stephanie. "These things take time."

In the other room, Beau's mother was coughing again.

"Beau is just like a nurse," I whispered.

"Shhh. He's coming back," said Stephanie, clearing her throat, getting ready for the big question. "I've never felt this jittery in all my life!"

Beau returned from the bedroom and walked past us to a cupboard by the sink.

"We've got some Coke," he said, rummaging around among the bottles and boxes in the cupboard. "No, there's no Coke, we're all out, I guess," he said. "Want some water? Or we can mix up some Kool-Aid."

Stephanie and I looked at each other.

"Really, no," said Stephanie. "But thanks any-

151

way. It's really getting late. I told Mother we'd be right back."

There was a long silence. Beau's hair was bleached straw color from working in the sun, and his arms were brown against his white shirt. Why doesn't she ask him? I thought. I looked over at Stephanie. She was twirling her wristwatch.

"Did you come over here for anything special?" asked Beau, trying again. Arms folded, he was leaning against the sink. He seemed much more relaxed on his home territory than he did at our house.

"Oh, no," faltered Stephanie, "we just wanted to see how you were doing."

"Stephanie!" I said.

"Well, yes, I mean, no. That is, there was something, wasn't there." Beau was watching her with curiosity. Stephanie took a deep breath. Her voice wobbled.

"You see, there's a party at our church on Saturday, and I, that is, Lou and I were wondering if you'd like to go. With us, I mean. Mother will drive us there of course. Seven thirty. Nothing fancy. You don't have to dress up or anything. Of course, if you're busy or something . . ."

The silence was deafening. We waited for Beau to say something. He was staring at the hole in the toe of his sneaker.

It throws boys off guard when you spring it on them sudden like that. When Marty had asked Alfred

Pinkham to take her to the sixth-grade dance, he looked like he'd been struck by lightning. Then he said in a loud voice, "Do I have to?" Marty didn't know what to say.

He's probably making up an excuse, I thought. That's what boys do half the time. I was waiting for Beau to say that he had to stay with his mother, or he had to wash the dog, or he'd promised to work overtime at the Farrells'. That's what you'd expect from an eighth-grade boy. Some dumb excuse.

But Beau fooled us. He stared at his shoe some more, and then a grin started dancing around the corners of his mouth. He looked up, and his grin turned into a real huge, full-fledged, honest-to-goodness smile.

"Hey, Ma!" Beau leaned into the doorway of the bedroom where his mother was resting. "Can I go to some church party on Saturday with the Berry girls? Seven thirty and they're driving?"

Stephanie beamed.

From the bedroom Mrs. Carney answered in a tiny voice, "Yes, how nice." Then she added that it was getting pretty dark outside, and Beau should walk us home with their flashlight.

The three of us set off in the darkness, the circle of light from Beau's flashlight picking out potholes in the road. The air was cool and biting, the breeze rustling the leaves in the shadowy trees. A few katydids rasped in the dry, brown weeds at the side of the road. Stephanie and Beau hardly said a word, so I did most of the talking, pointing out the constellations that I knew from camp—the Big Dipper and Cassiopeia and Cepheus. . . .

After a while we turned off the flashlight and gave ourselves the creeps, pretending the lumps of alder bushes were dragons, and the telephone poles giant spears. Beau held the flashlight under his chin and made monster noises, and Stephanie and I collapsed in a fit of giggles.

We were a few feet from the road that went into the Farrells' dump when Beau threw out his arm.

"Wait up!" he whispered. "Look! Over there! By the dump! There's a fire in the woods!"

CHAPTER THIRTEEN

"I knew it, Stephanie!" I said in a low voice. "Those tracks. I knew something was fishy!"

A large fire winked at us through the woods like a distant light burning in somebody's front window on a dark night. Trees loomed up between us and the fire, and the smell of burning leaves hung in the air.

"Somebody's in there," said Stephanie. "Maybe Mr. Farrell is burning his trash."

"At this time of night?" I said. It was almost nine o'clock.

"Wow! You could toast a few marshmallows over that fire!" muttered Beau. He walked a few steps into the dirt road, his flashlight playing over the dark tangle of trees and shrubs.

"Look! There's something over there!" I pointed to a big shadow farther down the road.

We moved closer together. Stephanie reached over and grabbed my hand. Beau's flashlight lit up a circle on the side of an empty car. There were the same red-and-gold letters we'd seen at the Farrells'—TO HELL OR BUST.

"It's Sonny!" I exclaimed.

"I'm going in there!" said Beau. "That fool is going to set the whole darned woods on fire if he's not careful!"

"Hey! You can't go by yourself," said Stephanie, grabbing his sleeve to hold him back.

But Beau shoved past her, head down low.

"Beau! Be careful!"

Stephanie held her hands to her cheeks and stared into the woods.

"It's dry as tinder in there. I'm going to get Father! Don't you move, Lou. Stay out by the road and keep watch."

She turned, and in an instant the night swallowed her up.

I hugged my arms together and waited at the end of the road. The fire was growing bigger. I could hear the dull roar of the flames.

Keep watch? What if Beau needs help? I thought. What if he gets hurt? Or Sonny? Father said Sonny had no common sense. I knew I had no choice. I ducked to keep the overhanging branches out of my eyes, and soon I was two steps behind Beau.

Beau whirled around. "Lou, you're crazy! Get out of here!"

"I'm no crazier than you are!" I shot back.

Twigs snapped softly under our feet, and the wind

swished in the trees. We could hear voices over the hissing of the fire. Smoke was heavy in the air. We inched forward on our hands and knees through the underbrush. The fire's glow cast eerie dancing shadows on Beau's face. His whole body was taut.

The dump appeared in the clearing, a mountain of trash, years of accumulated junk from the houses in the neighborhood. To one side Sonny and Clarence had pitched an old brown canvas tent. The ground was littered with sleeping bags, boots, bottles, tin cans, and water jugs. Between the tent and the trash pile the fire raged.

"Wow! Look at that fire!" Beau's voice was hoarse.

Ahead of us flames leaped up high in the air. Sparks popped and crackled in the darkness. Sonny and Clarence had pushed together a tight circle of rocks to enclose the fire, but in one spot the flames had escaped and were licking a steady path toward the woods.

Through the smoke we could see the boys, leaning against two old tree stumps, a beer bottle propped between them, loading a twenty-two. On a nearby log they had lined up a row of empty bottles.

"Hey, Sonny, I thought you was the world's greatest sharpshooter! Why, you couldn't hit a rabbit if it was settin' on your big toe!" Clarence bellowed with laughter.

"You keep joshing me, Clarence, and I'm liable to let my finger slip. Remember Drummer? That dog was in the wrong place at the wrong time."

Sonny took a wobbly aim and pulled the trigger. The bottle shattered, glass shards shooting off in all directions. He took aim at the next one.

My heart was pounding like a bass drum. A bush nearby burst into flame. Clarence and Sonny acted like this was a Sunday school picnic. They hardly noticed a thing.

"We've got to warn them, Beau! The flames are spreading fast!"

"Are you kidding? The Farrells are potted. That gun is loaded. We'd be sitting ducks!"

"Oh, Beau, what'll we do?" I whispered.

"I gotta think of something," said Beau again. There was a frightened edge to his voice that told me he was as scared as I was.

Just then we saw the fluttering crow, black as midnight against the blinding light of the fire.

"Oh, no!" My hand tightened on Beau's arm. "It's Crow!"

It had to be Crow. No other bird would be that crazy. Around and around he circled, slicing through the smoke, swooping inches over the boys, soaring upward, then down again into the light of the fire.

Clarence and Sonny sat bolt upright and stared in amazement.

"What in blazes . . . ?" muttered Sonny, scratching his head in disbelief. A slow smile spread over his face. His eyes narrowed.

"Clarence, my boy, guess what we're havin' for supper tonight?"

He reached for Crow with his bare hands, just missing as the bird shot by. Clarence laughed and slapped his knee. Sonny lurched to his feet. The second time Crow passed overhead he was ready. With sudden determination he grabbed him out of the air.

Crow fought back with all his strength, flapping his wings like fury and arching his neck in attack. He jabbed his bill at Sonny's face, but the boy shielded his eyes and held on tight.

"Get the gun!" he hollered to Clarence. "Finish him off!"

Clarence leaped up light as a cat, picked up the gun, and curled his finger around the trigger.

"Beau! They'll kill him!"

It was horrible. Clarence shouldered the twenty-two. Crow struggled desperately in Sonny's hands. I closed my eyes. Any instant I would hear the shot blowing poor Crow to smithereens.

"Get outta here, Lou!" shouted Beau.

The bushes rustled and Beau pushed past me. He hurled himself at the gun, knocking it to the ground. Clarence fell backward with a thud.

"What the devil!" said Sonny.

Crow burst from his arms. Sonny squinted into the night, waving the smoke away from his eyes.

"The woods!" shouted Beau wildly. "Quick! We've

got to keep the fire back from the woods!"

He grabbed a sleeping bag and pounded the flames. Dirt and sparks flew into the air. Smoke billowed around his head. The heat was intense.

"We done it this time, Sonny! Wow! We're in a real pickle!" moaned Clarence.

The water bottles were lying off to one side by the tent. Clarence fumbled with the tops and up-ended them over the flames. But it was like dousing a bonfire with teacups. The blaze had grown to the size of a school bus and roared like a freight train.

"Beat it down, Clarence!" yelled Beau holding up his shovel. "You got to beat it down!"

Clarence bashed at the fire with his sleeping bag.

"You stupid blockhead," shouted Sonny, staggering toward his brother. "I thought you was watching this fire!"

"Blame it on me, will ya'! Look out! The tent is about to catch!"

The tent ignited with a loud poof, then crumpled into itself like a burning newspaper.

I stripped off my jacket and swung it over my head like an ax, whacking down the flames. The ground under my feet was hot. Sonny grabbed an old board and squeezed in among us. I lost track of time. Over and over again we tried to stamp out the flames, but it seemed as soon as we got the fire out in one place, it would flare up in another. Behind us, a fir tree exploded with a thunderous roar.

Beau grabbed my arm. His face and arms were black with soot, and sweat poured down his forehead.

"Lou! Get your father! This blaze is out of control!"

"You come too!" I hollered back.

Beau shook his head. "Get going, Lou! We need help!"

I turned and fled, my feet racing over the ground, heading blindly for the main road. I tripped over a rock. Pain stabbed my foot like I'd stepped on barbed wire. I scrambled up again. I had to get Father before it was too late.

At our house the headlights of the Jeep flashed. Stephanie must have spread the alarm. Father was on his way. The Jeep lurched out of the driveway, the wheels squealing at the turn. I stood at the side of the road as Father whizzed by and turned into the dump.

"Oh, please, please let everything be all right," I prayed.

Tiny headlights crested the hill. A truck tore past our house and screeched to a halt. Men strapped Indian water pumps to their backs and dashed down the dirt road. A pickup carrying a huge water tank plunged into the woods. Mother must have called the Ellbridge Volunteer Fire Department.

"Circle round in back! The smoke's worse up here!" someone shouted.

"There's a brook just the other side of the house!"

"Get that car out of there before the gas tank explodes!"

"They said there's a couple of kids in there!"

"Hey, mister!" I tugged on a fireman's arm. "I'm one of the kids. I'm okay. But please hurry because—"

"Get back home to your ma, honey," said the man, shoving me aside as he rushed into the woods.

More firefighters clambered out of the cars and threw on heavy black coats. Flashlights danced in the darkness. The Ellbridge Fire Chief's car pulled up in the middle of the road, its light twirling like a lighthouse beacon. Sparky Grindle, the chief, scrambled out, barking orders and directing traffic.

Out of nowhere I saw Mr. Farrell's stooped figure coming toward me. His shoulders sagged.

"It's my boys again, right? Them two dimwitted sons of mine? I've had it. I'm too old for this."

"Oh, Mr. Farrell, I'm sure Sonny and Clarence will be all right. The firemen will get things under control." I hoped what I said was true.

"I kick 'em out of the house and where do they head? Across the road. With a couple of six-packs, I'll bet. Worse trouble than before."

Mr. Farrell muttered something under his breath and walked slowly toward the burning woods.

My foot was beginning to throb. I saw Mother hurrying toward me.

"Peewee, what a scare you gave us! What a scare! Thank God you're not hurt!"

She hugged me tight. Jennie and Stephanie appeared behind her. We huddled together in the night, our arms around each other. I told them what had happened in the woods. We talked about Crowberry and Beau and Father. Then we sat down on a rock by the side of the road. There was nothing to do but wait.

CHAPTER FOURTEEN

*A*fter that night there was no question about it. Beau was a hero. The Ellbridge volunteer firemen wanted him to sign up right there on the spot, but of course he was underage. Mr. Farrell gave him a twenty-five dollar reward. All the neighbors heard about it. The kids at school heard about it. Aunt Eleanor sent a postcard from California. It was exciting to think we knew someone as famous as Beau.

It took an hour for Sparky and his men to get the fire under control, and another half an hour to hose down the smoldering rubble. As we shivered in the night we could hear the whine of the pump truck, the shouts of men in the forest, and the scratchy police radio in Sparky's car. Someone bellowed instructions on a bullhorn. The smoke was thick as fog.

Mother, Stephanie, Jennie, and I waited by the road. We weren't worried, because one of the firemen came out and told us that nobody was hurt.

They were double-checking to make sure the fire was completely out. All the same it was a relief when Father and Beau came out of the woods.

At first I didn't recognize Beau in the dark, surrounded by a knot of firefighters straggling out to the main road. His shirt was torn, and his face looked as if he'd blackened it with cork for Halloween. But when I caught his eye, he grinned and gave the thumbs-up sign. The firemen gathered around the chief's car, its signal light still flashing.

"You almost had yourself a full-scale forest fire," Sparky said to Father and Mr. Farrell. "I think we held it to two or three acres in the end, don't you, Doc?"

"I don't know what we would have done without your boys," Father said, shaking his hand. "We have a lot to thank you for."

"You can thank that Carney boy for keeping it in the bag till we got here," Sparky said. "You done a great job, son."

Beau nodded his head. "Yes, sir, I thought we was finished for sure. You come along in the nick of time."

From his smile, I knew he was pleased. He wiped his face on the back of his sleeve, but it didn't do much but rearrange the dirt.

"Know what?" said Sparky. "I'm going to put in a call to the *Ellbridge American* first thing in the morning and have them write this up. We got us a real, genuine hero here."

Sparky thumped Beau on the back a couple of times.

Jennie came running over and grabbed Beau's hand.

"Oh, Beau," she said. "I just knew you wouldn't let Sonny and Clarence burn down the woods."

"Horace!" the chief called to his assistant, gesturing with his thumb toward the Farrell boys. "Take these boys into the station, will ya'? I'll meet you in there."

I peered into the darkness. I could barely make out Sonny's red-and-black shirt in the icy blue light from Sparky's car. Clarence shuffled along with his eyes fixed on the ground, but Sonny had come to life with a vengeance. He was waving his arms around, punching his fists into the air, carrying on as loud as a radio with the volume turned up too high. Mr. Farrell folded his arms across his chest, thrust out his chin, and glared.

"I tell you, Chief, it was this way. My brother Clarence here, who was in charge of the fire, got a little carried away—"

"Sure, sure, we know all about it, Sonny," said Sparky. "We'll write it up at the station. Now how was it that you two Boy Scouts happened to be having a weenie roast in the woods when the fire danger is sky high in every county in the state?"

"Well, now. I can explain all that. You see, it was like this, our radio conked out on us—"

"Anyone care for a good story? This guy lies like a rug!" somebody hollered.

"No, no, I tell ya', we thought we heard thunder off in the distance, like it was going to rain, so of course we weren't worried about—"

"That weren't no thunder, Sonny. That was Clarence belchin'!"

Everyone roared. Sonny was still explaining everything while Sparky ushered him and Clarence into the backseat of Horace's car.

"Drive these jokers into town," Sparky said to Horace. "I'm going to take this young fellow and his mother back home and get a few hard facts on the way."

"Ma? Is Ma here?" said Beau, looking around. "Geez. She'll freeze out here. She ain't supposed to leave the house."

Our eyes followed Beau's to Sparky's car. There, huddled in the backseat and wrapped up in a faded quilt like a papoose, was Mrs. Carney. Someone had driven over to the Carneys' to get her. Beau rushed over to his mother.

"Ma! What are you doin' here?"

He climbed into the car, nearly bumping his head on the door frame, and gave her a hug. When he pulled away, there was a big sooty smudge on his mother's cheek. The fire chief climbed into the driver's seat, and the crowd moved back to make room for the car.

" 'Bye, Beau!" yelled Jennie. "Next time you come over I'll trade my new baseball cards with you!"

"We'll call you tomorrow about the party!" shouted Stephanie. "Don't forget!"

I poked my head out between two burly firefighters who were part of a line along the road watching the chief's car pull away. I wished I was taller.

"Louise! You forgot something!"

I felt the cloth slam into my arms. It was my jacket, burned almost beyond recognition. I held it up and waved it at Beau. His finger and thumb curled around in an okay sign. His eyes were laughing through his black mask of soot. The car edged out onto the main road and drove away.

Father spoke a few words to Mr. Farrell. The old farmer slowly rubbed his forehead. He was going to follow the boys into town. The night was young, still enough time for Sonny and Clarence to get into more trouble.

When the chief's car had gone, I leaned on Mother's arm and limped to the Jeep, and we all drove home. Father examined my foot, which was pretty sore, and gave me a tetanus shot. Mother made up an ice pack. I was filthy. The ring of soot around the tub was as black as Oreo cookies. After my bath Jennie sat on the edge of my bed and wanted to hear about Sonny and Clarence and the fire a thousand times, and then she wanted to hear it all over again.

We couldn't wait to get to town the next day and

tell all the kids about our forest fire. When Beau's picture appeared in the *Ellbridge American* the day after that, we were fit to be tied. His hair was parted neatly on one side, and somebody had found him a shirt and tie for the picture. He seemed way older than fourteen. I had to look twice to make sure it was really him. They mentioned our names in the paper too. Mother ordered extra copies for all our relatives, and some for Beau's, too. If Mr. Muldoon recognized Beau from the picture, he never said a word.

When Beau showed up at the church party on Saturday, the kids buzzed around him like flies. He told the story of the fire three times to every single person there—what Sonny and Clarence said, how the tent went up like a torch, and how the cuffs on his pants were completely burned off. He danced with Stephanie and he danced with me and he drank about a gallon of Mr. Munson's Super-Special-Bug-Juice Punch.

Mother was late coming to pick us up. We waited out in front of the church, knocking our feet together to keep up the circulation. It was almost cold enough to see your breath. The parking lot was empty. The store lights on Main Street twinkled off in the distance. We huddled together on the wooden steps of the church and looked at the stars. We talked about the church party and then we talked some about Beau's mother and then we fell silent.

"Beau, there's something I've been meaning to ask you," said Stephanie finally, hugging her knees to keep warm. "You don't have to tell us if you don't want to."

Oh, no, I thought. She's going to ask him about the twenty dollars. Just the way I did. The lettuce patch all over again.

"What is it?" asked Beau.

"Well, I know it's none of my business," said Stephanie. She stopped.

"And?"

"I don't want you to think I'm prying or anything."

"So what is it?"

"You won't get mad at me?"

"I promise I won't get mad."

"Well, I've just got to know. Why did you steal those groceries from the A&P?"

Beau was silent. The clock on the town hall struck ten.

"I mean, it wouldn't make the slightest difference to me if you had a good reason or not. It wouldn't matter at all, really. I was just wondering."

"I don't know," said Beau. "I know it's not right, stealing stuff. I wish I could explain what makes me do it. I guess I get thinking . . . Ma and Pa are human. They need something decent to live on, just like everyone else."

I thought of Beau's mother coughing to exhaustion

night after night. How would I feel knowing there wasn't any money to pay for medicine, knowing life could be made easier with a stack of new magazines, the pages crisp and fragrant, or a few extra cans of tuna fish in the cupboard, just in case the mice got into the potatoes?

And Beau's father, not pushing exactly, not asking straight out, but just hinting, that it sure wouldn't hurt any if he had a new pair of shoes, size eleven, and preferably with rawhide laces and good thick soles. Beau never took anything for himself.

"But stealing is wrong," said Stephanie. "It's taking something that belongs to somebody else."

"I know it's wrong," said Beau. He was quiet for a long time. Then he said very low, "What would you do if you saw your mother dying right before your eyes? And you didn't have but two dollars for food?"

"I don't know what I'd do in your situation," said Stephanie softly. "I guess sometimes people make up their own rules. It must be awful, stealing."

"It is," said Beau. "I feel sick as a dog when I'm taking stuff."

Beau's face was pale in the glow of the lonely streetlight. His eyes were dark and sorrowful. In the distance, the Union River swirled under the Main Street bridge with a melancholy roar.

"You mean you've stolen stuff before?" asked Stephanie.

Beau didn't answer her. I think Stephanie already knew the answer. For a moment we sat there in silence, each of us lost in thought.

"They try so hard, and they don't have a thing to show for it," Beau said softly.

"They've got you, Beau," I whispered.

"Wow," Beau laughed. "Big deal."

"No, I mean it," I said. "I wish I had you in my family. It would be wonderful."

My ears grew warm. I was glad it was dark so no one could see me. I was beginning to sound like a moonstruck idiot. Suddenly it struck me. I loved Beau and I *didn't care* if he was a thief or not. I didn't care if he'd taken a million dollars or twenty dollars or the top of a tube of toothpaste. And somehow I could tell he knew I felt that way.

Beau stood up. He stretched, and then he reached out and pulled Stephanie and me to our feet. I couldn't be absolutely sure, but I think, I really think, he squeezed my hand.

Stephanie blew on her fingers in the frosty air.

"Hey, your mother is late," said Beau.

"The party probably let out early," said Stephanie. "That's why. Beau, you want to come to the regular fellowship meeting next week?"

"The kids will kill us if we don't bring you again," I said, trying to get the conversation back to where my heart would calm down. "You've got to come."

"Okay. I will. It was fun tonight," he said.

Mother's car veered around the corner and pulled up in front of the church. All the way home, Mother talked to Beau about his parents, and his job at the Farrells', and how their garden was growing, and what he would be taking in school this year. He sat up front, and Stephanie and I sat silently in the backseat. When he got out of the car, he thanked us again. Bozo was barking his head off, so you could hardly hear a word.

"Do you think Beau will ever change, Mother?" asked Stephanie after we left Beau. "Quit stealing for good, I mean?"

Mother pulled the car into our driveway and turned off the motor. "In my experience, most people change very little," she said. "But a few do."

"What about Beau?" I asked.

"I have a lot of hope for Beau," said Mother softly. "He's a pretty tough character. Yes, I think there's a very good chance he's one of the few."

CHAPTER FIFTEEN

"I'll think of a way to get him back. Don't you worry, Jen," said Stephanie. She was talking about Crowberry. He'd been missing for a week.

It was April. A lot had happened since the fire. Jennie was settled into kindergarten. Beau had been going to Youth Fellowship all winter long. Stephanie got her braces off and I got mine on. But the biggest change had happened to Crowberry.

He still chased the chickens and teased Micky and wheeled overhead between the barn and the house. But ever since the fire, whenever we called him, he simply wouldn't come. We tried everything, hollering until we were hoarse, clattering the dog food can with a spoon, sneaking up under his tree. After the fire Crow decided that people were no good, and he wouldn't have a thing to do with us. Finally we just gave up trying.

We got busy with school. I won another prize at the Jaycees' Halloween party with my cannibal costume. I taped real chicken bones under my nose. We invited Dr. Butler for Thanksgiving dinner, and after the dishes were cleared away, we took him out to the old pine tree and showed him Crow's perch at the top. He said there was nothing we could do but hope the bird would forget about the fire, but to be honest, he was surprised Crow had stayed with us this long.

At Christmas we went caroling with Beau and the Youth Fellowship to the county jail down the street from the church. There were only two prisoners in the jail. We couldn't see them, but after we finished "Silent Night," we could hear their isolated clapping echo through the windowless halls. For a second I wondered whether it might be Sonny and Clarence in jail because of the fire, but I knew it couldn't be. Right after the fire Mr. Farrell had made them sign up for the Marines. If the boys were still stirring up trouble, the people in South Carolina had to worry, not us.

Throughout the winter we'd catch glimpses of Crow. We scattered grain over the frozen snow under his tree. Once, in an awful blizzard, he huddled outside against the window for two whole days. Sometimes he'd disappear for a week at a time. But he always came back. One morning in early spring Jennie called us excitedly to the window.

"Hey! Two crows, everybody! There are two crows in Crowberry's tree!"

Sure enough. Crow had found himself a friend. We watched through the binoculars as one of the crows flew to a branch and waited. A minute later the second landed on the branch above and began dancing and fluffing its feathers, trying to get the first crow's attention. He seemed to have something for her in his beak. You didn't have to be a genius to figure out what was going on.

"Do you think Crowberry has a girlfriend?" asked Jennie.

"Maybe Crow was a girl all this time and has a boyfriend," I said. "But whatever's going on, they're both happy."

Crow acted head over heels in love. He strutted back and forth, bobbing his head and puffing his feathers, hoping his mate would notice. Sometimes he made weird rattling noises, different from his usual sound. And if a third crow approached, probably another male, he tried to fight him off, flying headlong into the other bird to keep him away from his tree.

"Crowberry is acting like a real jerk!" said Jennie.

"No, he's not," said Stephanie. "He's trying to make a good impression."

One day we noticed the tree was empty. The next day was the same. After a week went by, we decided to initiate an official search. Stephanie and I spent the better part of a Saturday morning hooting and hollering, "Here, Crowberry! Here, Crowberry!" We walked past the Farrells' and all the way to the Carneys'. We tramped across the fields to the river and searched the woods around the dump. But Crow and his mate were gone for good. One day followed another. There was no sign of them. We didn't even see anything that might be a nest.

Jennie was heartbroken.

"I told you, Jen, I'll think of a way to get him back," said Stephanie.

"What are you going to do?" I asked, wondering how Stephanie could always be so sure of herself.

"First we're going to tie dog food cans in the pine tree."

"Oh, yeah?" I said.

"And then we're going to paint some eggs to look like crow eggs. We'll fix up a fake nest. That might lure him back."

"How do you know what crow eggs look like?" I said.

"I don't," said Stephanie. "I'm leaving it up to you. You're the research department."

"What am I supposed to do?" asked Jennie eagerly. "I want to help too."

"You're going to walk over to the Carneys' and ask if we can borrow their extension cords. They've got tons. I've seen them in the back of the truck."

"What are the extension cords for?" asked Jennie.

"You'll see," said Stephanie. "Ask Beau to come over and help too. We'll need everybody."

I hunted through all our bird books, but none of them told about eggs.

"Well, then. Paint them light brown with black speckles. That's what I'd hatch if I were a crow," said Stephanie.

We carried the ladder out to the pine tree. Stephanie hung five cans of dog food from the branches like Christmas tree ornaments. Then we pushed some sticks together on a bough and cradled a half dozen painted eggs in the nest. One rolled out and broke on the ground.

"I don't think this is going to work, do you, Stephanie?" I said doubtfully.

"Of course it's not going to work, dummy," she said. "We're not doing this because it might work."

"We're not?" I said.

"No, Louise. We're doing it to help Jennie. She'll never get over the fact Crowberry has left us if we don't pretend we're trying to get him back. You remember how upset she was over Buffy, the sea gull."

"So you don't think he's coming back?" I said.

"Of course not. Why would he want to come back? He's found a girlfriend. It's time to move on. Now climb up that ladder and see if you can see Beau and Jennie. I'm going to get the record player."

I mounted the ladder halfway up and shaded my eyes against the sun. It was a beautiful spring morning. The song sparrows were singing, and the Wor-

178

den River sparkled in the sun. Tiny shoots of green poked up through the dead winter grass. Pretty soon I saw Beau and Jennie coming down the road. They were running. Beau had a coil of extension cord looped over his shoulder.

"Can you hook the cord up to the record player, Beau?" called Stephanie. "We want to set it up under Crow's tree."

Beau began unwinding the cord, stretching it across the field between the house and Crow's tree.

"What are we doing this for?" Jennie asked in a cheerful voice. "Do you really think it will make Crowberry come back?"

"It's certainly worth a try," said Stephanie, catching my eye knowingly. "Now as soon as Beau has everything ready, we'll get the bird call record and set it to play the crow section. Then we'll keep lifting the needle and playing that part over and over again."

"At top volume," I said.

"Right, Louise," said Stephanie. "At top volume. And then Crowberry may hear it and decide to come back."

Beau cupped his hands to his lips and called from the center of the field, "That's it, Stephanie. The cord won't reach any farther."

"What the heck," said Stephanie. "That's probably far enough. Okay, everybody, let's start the record and see what happens."

We all gathered on a blanket in the grass around

the phonograph. Stephanie helped Jennie find the right band on the record. Beau propped himself on one elbow next to Jennie, a smile hovering on his lips.

"American crow," intoned the stern-voiced narrator on the record. *"Caw . . . caw . . . caawww. Caw . . . caw . . . caawwww."*

"That's it, Jen. Run it through again," said Stephanie. "Now look around. Anybody see Crowberry?"

We must have played the crow section fifty times before Jennie looked up sadly and said, "It's not going to work. Crowberry's gone for good. He's not coming back." Tears filled her eyes and her lips trembled.

Beau sat up, crossing his legs Indian-style and pulling Jennie onto his lap. "Hey, Jen, that old Crowberry has to do things his own way. He can't live with people all the time. He wants to live with other crows."

"Otherwise the other crows will think he's weird," I said.

"Old Crowberry wants to get out there in the big wide world and start a family. Next year at this time you'll look up and see all his children flying around. Year after that, his grandchildren." He brushed away Jennie's tears with the back of his hand.

"And cousins, and nieces, and nephews," added Stephanie.

"Why, they'll be flying around that big old white house and red barn, saying, 'Where's that little girl old Uncle Crowberry told us about? Where's Jennifer Berry?' "

"Jennifer *Edith*—" said Jennie.

"Yeah. 'Jennifer Edith Berry. That girl who raised me. And let me tell you, can that girl do tricks.' That's what he's telling them. Old Crowberry's telling them to watch you."

"He is?" said Jennie. Her eyes were wide as saucers.

"Yep. He's telling them to watch you do that one-footer on the swing set. And that great backward somersault. And, 'Dang it all,' he's saying, 'you should see that girl jump rope.' "

Beau winked at us over Jennie's head. All of us were following Beau's story with rapt attention.

"Hey, I stink at jumping rope," said Jennie.

"Oh, it ain't *this* year, Jen," said Beau. "This is next year. And the year after that. You'll be red-hot skipping rope by then."

Jennie's smile broadened.

"Yes, sir, Crowberry'll tell them to keep an eye on you. Because there ain't no girl in Maine can do tricks as good as Jennifer Edith Berry, and that's a fact!"

Jennie beamed triumphantly. She turned around in Beau's lap, stood up, and putting her arms around his neck, gave him a big bear hug. Beau hugged her back, and they both fell onto the grass.

Suddenly Jennie pulled away. Her eyes grew round and she stared at Beau's chin.

"Beau, you got whiskers!"

"Jennifer Berry! That's rude!" exclaimed Stephanie. "We don't make personal remarks about somebody's appearance!"

Beau flushed, reached up, and rubbed his chin.

"That's right, Jen," he said, red with embarrassment. "You better listen to your big sister. That's Calvert's top graduate over there."

Stephanie giggled. We all laughed. Beau scooped Jennie up and swung her around by her wrists. Then we picked up some pinecones and pitched them at the dog food cans. Beau hit the fake bird's nest with a rock and the last five eggs dropped down with a splat. We let the phonograph record run on through the nuthatches and vireos until it finally got stuck on the purple bunting and played the same bird song over and over again. I guess we forgot about Crow. Finally Beau coiled up the extension cord and carried the record player back to the house. Mother asked him to stay for lunch. Crowberry never came back.

I'll never forget that morning, because the very next day Mr. Carney called up to tell us that they would be moving in a couple of weeks. He explained that Mrs. Carney thought she'd get her strength back faster if she lived nearer her family. So the Carneys were heading down south.

It was sad when Beau Carney left. I can hardly remember what happened. I just didn't want to think about it, I guess. After Beau and his parents moved, the windows of their house were boarded up, and somebody put up a big ugly sign by the driveway saying, "NO TRESPASSING." Nobody cut the grass anymore. Weeds grew up around the toilet in the front yard, hiding it in a tangled mass of green.

Every so often Mrs. Carney wrote us. Once Beau sent us his picture. He was sitting at the wheel of a tractor on his uncle's farm, squinting into the sunlight, his hair in his eyes. He looked happy. On the back of the picture he had written in neat, penciled letters: "To the best girls I ever knew. Wish you were here. Love, Beau."

After that we received two or three more letters before they stopped coming. Mother said that sometimes that's what happens when neighbors move away. The Carneys probably got so busy with their new life, they didn't have time to write. But she was sure Beau wouldn't forget us. People remember the happy moments in their lives forever.

Mother was right. I can picture Beau Carney tossing sticks to Crowberry clear as if it all happened yesterday. I'll never forget how those two strays became part of our lives.

Years later, after my parents had sold the farm and moved into town, I went back to see the place. The Carneys' house was no longer standing, and

Lloyd Farrell's barn was a gift shop. Our own barn was gray and sagging with neglect, but our house had been rebuilt and was painted bright yellow. The present owner said he didn't mind if I walked around the property, so I set off through the back field, overgrown with sweet fern and blueberry bushes. When I got to Crowberry's pine tree, I sat down underneath it in the fragrant pine needles, leaning my back against the trunk, sticky with sap.

I recalled that spring day long ago when the old tree had been decorated with a homemade nest and dog food cans. Running my hand over the moss, I thought of the fun Stephanie, Jennie, and I used to have making tiny villages in the forest floor, digging up mounds of emerald green for front lawns and dotting the roads with little stick fence posts and white pebble stone walkways.

Gazing over the field, I remembered how Beau had sent the chickens scurrying through the grass with the bugle, the day of the circus.

Absentmindedly, I picked up a rock and scraped away the pine needles. And there, hidden at the base of the tree where Crow had spent so many days and nights, tucked between two lichen-covered rocks and torn and faded almost beyond recognition, was a twenty-dollar bill.

90-174

DATE DUE

F
Wi

Wild, Elizabeth

Along came a black
bird

DATE DUE	BORROWER	
OCT 25	Bryn	22
MAY 22	Jenny	4
EB 5	Shannon	23
	Alix	13

90-174

F
Wi

Wild, Elizabeth

Along came a black
bird

93